NINETY-TWO IN THE SHADE

Thomas McGuane is the author of six other novels: *The Sporting Club*; *The Bushwhacked Piano*; *Panama*; *Nobody's Angel*; *To Skin a Cat*; and *Something to Be Desired*; and a collection of pieces, *An Outside Chance: Essays on Sport*. He lives in Montana on a cattle and quarter-horse ranch. *The Sporting Club* and *Panama* are also available in the Penguin Contemporary American Fiction Series.

Thomas McGuane

NINETY-TWO IN THE SHADE

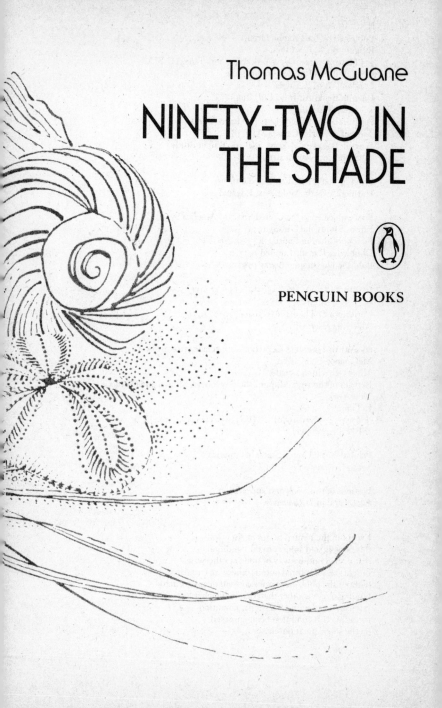

PENGUIN BOOKS

PENGUIN BOOKS
Published by the Penguin Group
Penguin Books USA Inc.,
375 Hudson Street, New York, New York 10014, U.S.A.
Penguin Books Ltd, 27 Wrights Lane,
London W8 5 TZ, England
Penguin Books Australia Ltd, Ringwood,
Victoria, Australia
Penguin Books Canada Ltd, 10 Alcorn Avenue,
Toronto, Ontario, Canada M4V 3B2
Penguin Books (N.Z.) Ltd, 182–190 Wairau Road,
Auckland 10, New Zealand

Penguin Books Ltd, Registered Offices:
Harmondsworth, Middlesex, England

First published in the United States of America by
Farrar, Straus and Giroux 1973
First published in Canada by
Doubleday Canada Limited 1973
Published in Penguin Books 1980

20   19   18   17   16   15   14   13   12   11

LIBRARY OF CONGRESS CATALOGING IN PUBLICATION DATA
McGuane, Thomas.
Ninety-two in the shade.
Reprint of the 1973 ed. published by Farrar, Straus, and Giroux,
New York.
I. Title.
[PZ7.M1475Ni   1980]   [PS3563.A3114]   813'.5'4
ISBN 0 14 00.9907 7

Printed in the United States of America
Set in Janson

Portions of this book first appeared in
Fiction and in *TriQuarterly*.

for Beck for Beck for Beck

*"Man is excellently made
and eagerly lives the kind of life that is being lived."*

MIKHAIL ZOSHCHENKO

NINETY-TWO IN THE SHADE

NOBODY KNOWS, FROM SEA TO SHINING SEA,

why we are having all this trouble with our republic ...

Riding home from Gainesville with four people,

Thomas Skelton was in a globe of his own hallucinatory

despair, a little blown away it is true; but nothing quite

as serious as that sense of internal collapse and loss almost

of armature that made it increasingly difficult to so

much as sit up straight.

Skelton, two men, two women, wound up in a white

clapboard hotel near Homestead frequented by citrus

pickers; and a long night began of streaks, halos, and

comas. Toward its end, Skelton found himself sitting on

3

an enormous expanse of gleaming wood floor. He could see no furniture and the walls were yielding. He seemed to be alone; and he came to wonder what was becoming of him. There was a liquid window filling with silver light; and just over the sill he could see the crown of a palm tree moistly easing itself into his view. Thus he knew he was on the second floor. He turned over on his side and heard the change in his pocket ring out on the hardwood floor. There were voices in fatigue cadences, movement below, and vague, humming vibrations in the joists.

He got to his feet and moved upon the region of the window. There was an empty intersection and a traffic light that changed colors in mid-air at lazy, musical intervals. The red was rather penetrating and Skelton closed his eyes when he saw it coming.

The voices were flying from the bathroom. Skelton left the window and traversed the vague space of the empty room to the voice-filled doorway. In the bathroom a terrible fluorescence curved over the surfaces of the plumbing. The four people were standing naked in the tub with the lurid fluorescence all over them. One of the men was bending over and squeezing his hands between his knees. The other man leaned up against the wall behind the tub as though waiting to board a bus or to light a blonde's cigarette in a 1947 movie. The two women were heating something in a screw-on bottle cap over a Zippo. The tub rested on iron frog's feet.

Skelton studied himself until he was sure that he was dressed and slipped out of the hotel. He walked to Homestead, then right on through town, tripping his brains out in the emptiness of 5 a.m. His feet were making an awful clatter on the pavement. When he got to the far side of town, he felt a small pain in his stomach.

He touched himself and discovered a short heavy gun in his waistband, a .38 Colt Cobra. What in the hell was that doing there. He took it out and threw it into a mosquito ditch and walked on. Then he couldn't believe that there had ever been a gun; so he walked back to the mosquito ditch and saw it lying on the bottom, hard and brilliant in the stagnant slime.

The trees along the road were full of catbirds. Skelton kept on. It was getting warm and he could begin to smell the blacktop. Then the intersection of A1A and the sign to Key West. He stuck out his thumb and thought, They won't see I'm insane until I'm already in the car. It is hot and when I get to Key West I'll borrow some money and order a beverage. I'll get a six-pack and take my skiff out on the reef. If they say in the car that I am insane, I will take over the wheel.

No one said he was insane; neither the hardware salesman, the United Parcel driver nor the crawfisherman who drove the last leg into Key West suggested such a thing. When Skelton told the hardware salesman that the paint had just lifted off the whole car in a single piece, the hardware salesman agreed with him about how Detroit put things together. This was the epoch of uneasy alliances.

The sun penetrated the blue-green sea over the reef in shafts like church light clear to the reef. Schools of bait were on the reef like some vast gleaming silver pointillism shifting suddenly when predators passed through, then re-forming around the invisible trajectory of the vanished assailant. Skelton drifted over the millionfold expanse of the bait school calming down and finishing his six beers at some speed. More pelagic fish were finding the bait, and as they drove up under it, sheets of silver erupted from the sea scattering with the noise of heavy rain. The gulls came then by the tens and twenties and dropped everywhere among the bait, heavy and singular.

When the bait was gone and Skelton was drifting once more in the wooden skiff over the stony, illuminated reef, he saw that he would have to find a way of going on.

CARTER HAD A SKIFF LIKE NICHOL DANCE'S BUT where Carter's would high-center on a shallow bank Nichol's would pole in dew and let him drop in those little basins where the fish held faced up tide on the incoming water.

Now it was Dance's system to fish by the tide like a sniper and time his stops so the fish would come to him or to his chum slick; where Faron Carter fished the flats in the old style poling the skiff from the bow on the edge of the flats in the early flood then dropping back to the mangroves on the high water and looking for the waking fish.

But Dance knew the intersections and only touched the pole to set the skiff up and slip the anchor; or to chase a hooked fish in water too shallow to run the engine in. He made twice as many stops in a day as Carter and fished more by his brain as it was his method to be on the money when the fish came in on the moving water. So, Dance not only saw the flat from the top, but he saw it in cross section; because where the troughs were, the little sand streaks in the turtle grass, that is where the earliest fish came.

But on those days on the young moon or when a tide forced him to fish falling water, he was less skillful in poling out a bad situation to find what fish there were.

So, when Tom Skelton decided to guide, he knew it

was these two men that he would study; because theirs were the styles that there were. The other men at the dock were averages of Carter and Dance without either edge.

Now Carter was a level person who presented certain civic virtues that could not be ascribed to Dance. Carter could spend the day in the boat with well-known golfers charming them with articulate fishing stories. While Dance would brood about the tide or lose his temper; or, much the worst, begin drinking. The two men were similarly successful as guides over the long haul. Day after day, Carter put a sound amount of fish on the dock. While Dance, the incessant addict of long shots, would sometimes blank out entirely, coming home in an empty skiff black in the face; but on his best days he would produce fish in quantities incomprehensible to Carter. Skelton favored Dance.

Nichol Dance was in one or two ways an interchangeable creature, born in Center, Indiana, in 1930.

Twelve years ago he inherited the hardware store in Center and a woodlot six miles away full of buckeyes that stank in the spring. It took him six months to piss away half of what had been left him; hunting coons and drinking with his and his father's friends, he was picking up everybody's tabs. His sister who had married a Croatian foundryman from Gary tried to sue him out of the rest; but he hung on to what was about now the price of a new Ford, made a trip to Kentucky to buy a redbone bitch and bought a tavern instead.

One year later, in hazy circumstances, he shot and killed an exercise boy of forty from Lexington; and was run out of town.

For many years he carried that handgun, a rather esoteric Colt's "Bisley" model, with Mexican ivory grips showing eagles killing snakes, chambered for the army issue .45. The exercise boy had acted up, true enough; but the Colt made what is called short work of him, about what a two-iron would do to a deliquescent toadstool.

He traded the deed to the bar for a two-door Fairlane convertible and drove to the sea thinking that would be the spot to start over. He hit the beach at Hampton Roads, a brake drum binding the wheel in a sleet storm; picked up Route 1 and turned south till it ran out in Key West.

He'd driven those many miles without any terminal mechanical trouble, but on Southard Street in Key West the brake drum had had enough and caught fire. Burning rubber and oil from the brake line slowly worked into the Fairlane proper which was loaded down with belongings including a Motorola TV, the pistol in hand, and a case of government ammunition. Nothing to do but stand back and watch her go. When the flame reached eight feet over the sputtering convertible top, the ammunition began to fire; and then the television let go. Dance had the Bisley Colt in the top of his pants underneath a palm-leafed sport shirt he bought in St. Augustine and great alligator tears swam down his cheeks. The truth was he felt free as a bird.

A burning Ford full of things that blow up does draw a crowd. And the conchs—as the old-time white people of Key West are called—the conchs who saw Dance for the next month drove him crazy, toothlessly following him around and saying, "There he is! That'n's the one whats car caught afire!"

A couple of weeks of this and Dance began to wheel on them. He thought, I've got to scatter these bastards. They look like they'd eat you up some dark night.

Then odd jobs, hanging out at the dock, doing things for guides like Faron Carter, sandblasting flamingos on glass shower doors, substituting and finally guiding. And all along thinking about that exercise boy, once every year or so nearly getting to the point about that exercise boy that he nearly gave himself the same as he gave him, as a matter of restitution, as a matter of symmetry and as the one response to that fatal perfidy that put him and the exercise boy on the opposite sides of that empty bar, the deed to which was the final trace of a family business and a woodlot—integers of a winding-down life.

Then, a fifty-seven-day bad marriage to a Catholic from Chokoloskee that ended in the court reconciling everything he had acquired but a skiff and it all went off in a Bekins moving van with the wife up front by the driver, headed for the Everglades. And drinking of the kind that is a throwing of yourself against the threshold of suicide though lacking that final will to your own ceasing, without which all the hemlock and Colt's patented revolvers are of no more avail than ringside tickets, photostats of lost deeds, or snapshots of Granddad's five-bottom plow.

NICHOL DANCE'S GUIDE BOAT, "BUSHMASTER," was nosed up the tidal creek that bisected Grassy Key, not anchored but rammed into the red mangrove roots in a canopy of mosquitoes and sand flies. Nichol Dance's whole end of the creek smelled of whiskey. The ship-to-shore radio was turned on to the broadcast band; and out of its crackling loudspeaker, someone advised the prostrate Hoosier to "think young." Dance lay there, vaguely alive, his brain curing like a ham.

Carter shut the engine down and the two looked at Dance's person and found neither bullet holes nor seepage and knew as they had known in advance that he had polluted himself once more with one of the fifths that he always stored in the live wells. But, Tom Skelton thought, the intention to kill himself, however garbled or interfered with, was quite enough.

"Get in and see can you start the mother," said Carter.

Tom Skelton climbed aboard the *Bushmaster* and lowered the engine with the power tilt control up forward. With the electrical hum of its motor, Nichol Dance began to stir. Tom Skelton forgot himself for the moment, forgot the rather lurid momentary circumstance and felt only his own fine tremble to be that of the boat when, choked and started, the powerful engine passed its life through the craft and sent fine lapping tremors out around itself into the tidal creek.

Nichol Dance sat up and announced that he wanted a career in show business, with an air of having had one in an earlier life. Chemical impact thickened the flesh around his eyes. On the floor of the skiff was the Colt's patent revolver with Mexican ivory grips; and on his chest, his flowered shirt bore the print of the pistol.

Dance's uncanny presence produced a momentary silence in which the dry velocities of birds could be heard in the brushy creek. Even the bubbling of crustaceans on the red mangrove roots around him and the slow tidal seepage seemed to rise a measure or so while Nichol Dance looked them over with the same remote gaze you would understandably associate with the recently raised dead.

"A person can scarcely be deliberate any more," he said.

"What seems so exclusive to you about that," Carter inquired.

"Does it need to be exclusive for me to bring it up?"

"Not unless you're offering a franchise."

"You're the Skelton kid that's always on the god-damn flat in front of me."

"That's right," Skelton said positively to this basilisk drunk.

"I wonder how come."

"I enjoy water sports would be just about exactly how come."

"Very good. But child, I can't recommend it."

"I wasn't applying for a recommendation," Tom Skelton said.

"I was explaining," Dance said, "about how unattractive a day on the water can come to be."

"But I'd of known," Tom Skelton said, "that a person would spoil a boat trip if he only went out to shoot himself."

"Now look here, fucker, I didn't come here to be sassed—"

"Neither did I."

Nichol Dance picked up the Colt's patent revolver and discharged it into the mangroves all around Tom Skelton with a collective noise that was close to that of war.

"*Fucker*," he said, "*I don't seem to have your attention!*"

Carter said, "You have rattled the boy. Now let's just all of our selfs unwind and go home. And Nichol, that pistol has gotten to be a liability."

And Dance said to Carter, "But we've kept so many from crowding our trade, it discourages me to come acrosst a hard case." Then he smiled radiantly.

"I'm not a hard case, whatever that is. I am going to guide is all."

Nichol Dance stared a moment at Tom Skelton with only mildly drunken appreciation. He said, "Then why don't you do the little thing?"

"I think he means to," said Carter. "Now let's run before the sun sets."

Nichol Dance said to Carter, "Let him lead us, Cart."

Well, all right. Skelton reversed the engine, eased backward in the narrow marshy quarters past Carter who followed backing after him, the sandy turbulence on the creek bottom lifting and carrying down tide. Dance sat at ease in one of the fighting chairs, his face still blurred, but the impression of durability remained in the compression ridges of flesh under his eyes. Otherwise, Nichol Dance was just a displaced bumpkin run out of his own unmortgaged bar for shooting a man in the horse business through the wishbone in not quite disputable self-defense; part of the world of American bad actors who, when the chips are down, go to Florida with all the gothics and grotesqueries of chrome and poured-to-form concrete that that implies.

When Tom Skelton had running room, a nicety of judgment based on a precise guess of distance between propeller and ocean bottom, he put the skiff up on a plane and ran the shallow bank on a dead course for the Harbor Keys, then swung abruptly southwest on the crawfishermen's wheel track—a wandering trough perhaps two feet wide—which at this tide was absolutely the only way to cross the bank that separated them from Key West. Nichol Dance turned his head on a dark and sun-wrinkled neck to look at Carter and raise his eyebrows. Skelton centered the bow on the stacks of Key West Electric and started home.

Winter ducks and cormorants got up in front of the approaching skiffs and made off at angles to the boats' running course. Sea fans, coral heads, yellow cap rock, stone-crab and crawfish pots were inordinate and clear in the shallow water. The trap markers were affixed to

Clorox-bottle floats that hung down tide on yellow lines; but Skelton by painful and slow process knew very well how to run the country having slept out in mosquito bogs for his misjudgments. He had poled the better parts of full days upwind and up tide with bent drive shafts and wiped-out propellers for having had on the map of his brain previously unlocated coral heads or discarded ice cans from commercial boats; or for having lost surge channels in the glare crossing shallow reefs.

Well astern now, on Mente Chica Key, the outline of a bat tower could be seen against the smeared and windless sky.

"Leave it at the fuel dock," said Dance now blearier than ever but still letting a thin devilish gas from slightly pursed lips evidence some dire bowel chemistry.

Roy Soleil, the dockmaster, stood beside the two pumps with a mild visual suggestion that he was the third. He made no move to throw them a line as Tom eased in and reversed the engines for an eggshell landing that lifted Dance's eyebrows once more. Behind them, Carter was just now mooring; and Tom Skelton's brain was tumid with uncommitted navigational errors.

"Why my God," said Roy, "the original survivor."

Nichol Dance did not look up but kept his reddening neck bent while he refueled the skiff.

"I mean, what makes folks keep signing up on these rescue missions?" Roy inquired. "Or is a rescue something every boy should have?"

When Nichol raised himself up to fix Roy with a baleful stare, Roy flushed very slightly but did not, you could see, deviate from his curious course.

"What ails you?" said Nichol Dance.

"Ails me?"

Roy, the dockmaster, twice Nichol Dance's size, with the fame of maddened rages on his side, said:

"Nichol, that is what I have been trying to touch upon."

Carter by this time saw even from his distance what was afoot exactly; but the interval, even from Skelton's proximate view, between releasing the gas pump and arriving on the dock with the ash-handled kill-gaff in hand was imperceptible. Skelton supposed there had been some prelude, even some subsequent move by the immense dockmaster; but Nichol Dance was sure with the gaff and the dockmaster was quickly down, neatly skewered between hip and short ribs; while Nichol Dance, standing over as he thrashed, gripped the hardwood handle with both hands and bore down as though to kill a snake. Nichol Dance said to Carter, "Call a doctor for this New Jersey arc-welder polack." Carter ran to the pay phone and Dance disempaled the dockmaster, who lay bleeding, glaring and holding himself in with laced fingers. Then to Skelton he said, "Better get some law in here too before I think to wind this bug fucker's clock."

He looked at Roy.

"Roy, I'd go to Raiford Prison over you, if I needed."

"I see that."

When Tom Skelton came back, they sat to wait. First the ambulance came and took off the dockmaster. Then Nichol Dance handed Skelton a ledger of his bookings and told him to use the skiff. "I will call you from the joint as to what cut from your proceeds would be usual."

"How did you pick me?"

"If I gave the bookings to Cart, I'd lose them. Anybody you'd guide I'm going to get back."

It was a messy beginning. Still, he could regard his start with no sense of incursion by the events that surrounded it. He had enormous hopes for the future. He considered: mucus egg congestions are related to radiant sea creatures via indecipherable links of change.

"I CAN REMEMBER," SAID SKELTON'S MOTHER, "that autumn so clearly because I was expecting you. A man from Sugarloaf had been stung to death by bees on one of the Indian mounds and they brought him into Key West. They took him right over to the newspaper and laid out the corpse on the steps of the old city hall to get some pictures, but a colored man's dog wouldn't stop howling and leave them be. So they threw the corpse into a Ford sedan and drove it to the funeral parlor. The face was as big as *that* with bee stings and the colored man's dog chased the car and wouldn't stop howling until his owner ran him off to the shrimp dock. The dog got down under the pilings and kept on howling. That night when the boats went out you could hear the howling over all those shrimpers' engines and your father went down and brought the dog home and put him in the cistern with five pounds of sirloin until the howling stopped."

Skelton, still and listening, felt himself to be moving through the house, the full vacancy of its rooms, thinking, So much has been lost. In this heat, every garbage pail is full of fish skeletons and this town smells of the special lizard stench of churches or catacombs; narcosis dying as slowly as the life that would replace it.

MIRANDA'S HALLWAY: A SPINDLY MAHOGANY end table to which the termites have had access for a hundred years sustains a green Mason jar with its lost patent numerals in heavy glass; and holding in its opaque vegetable water from the Keys Aqueduct, ribbed orange squash-blossoms in their delicately emblematic subdivision of light.

It was cool in there, a house holding a beloved woman, the aural penetrations of a Cuban side street and the Gulf of Mexico in an upper window.

Skelton perplexed himself as to how many dead had been transported through this hallway. If you had a specific answer to that, you would possess innumerable anecdotes about mortality with which to regale your friends; or if you had no friends, then to address to that not so finite darkness in which we are all corporate shareholders. The trick, finally, Skelton knew, was to keep them rolling in the aisles, saving the best one for last, about how we die and die and die.

What a thought. I am going to fuck my way out of this one. Miranda used to do reds, crossed her sevens, and had a Leo rising. She was Skelton's girl, a pretty thing whose long black hair carried behind her as she walked.

The wooden fan made no sound in the front room. The door to the bedroom was ajar. Skelton paused midway across the room and felt a rising cold pass up through him as he began to hear through the doorway the bed's rachitic sprung utterance. Skelton tried without amusing himself to think of this as an unspeakable pubic disaster. Pain. He stepped sideways very slightly and saw against that band of further space the writhing within; and could not keep himself from saying, ". . . Miranda . . ." so that the front-room quiet fell across everything like an eclipse.

"Tom?"

"Yes . . ."

"I'm making love. Wait out there till I'm through."

Skelton walked to the window as though riding a

thermal. Not able to stand in one place, he returned to the table, rifled through the sewing box, removed a small silver snuffbox, a pocket mirror, and a razor blade. He opened the snuffbox with trembling fingers and tapped out a little heap of cocaine on the mirror. He divided the pile and drew it out in two long thin white lines; blocked first one nostril, then the other, and drew the cocaine into each.

He leaned back into the chair and tuned his ears once again to the bed's noise, which seemed to open and close in the room, tenebrous as a bird's claw. But by the time his nose numbed and his throat seemed to not quite close any longer, it had come to seem that the bed was not unmusical. And once its noise had stopped, he shared the exhausted breathing and relief from within. Across the room, the tall window suspended a pure convexity of luminous air toward Skelton; and in the door he had entered was a bar of fluorescing sun. He began to imagine that he could feel Key West urge itself against the Atlantic like a ship of terrible slow movement. The chrysalis he sometimes felt inside was beginning to shed and stream quite lambently.

"Tom?"

"Ah, Miranda."

"Are you blown away?"

"A little."

"Because you were upset?"

"Yes."

"This is Michael."

"I'm sorry," said Michael.

"That's all right. Did you have a nice time?"

"Yes, very."

"Well, that's fine."

Michael said, "I've got a plane to make."

"Well, good to see you and it's fine with me that you had a nice time . . . and uh that there is a plane for you to make . . ."

"Thanks." A perfunctory kiss to Miranda and away with him. When he was gone, Miranda said, "You didn't fire anything?"

"Uh-uh. Couple blows of your coke. What's that noise?"

"Michael going out."

"Sounded like the house falling down."

"Tom, I had this incredible orgasm."

"Do I have to hear about your organism too?"

"Just this one. It was like a whole dream of sweet things to eat. I mean, it all came to mind. Spun sugar, meringue, whipped egg whites, and all these clear German cake icings—"

"How about when your chum shot off? Was it a blintz or an omelet?"

"Ask him." She held Skelton's head standing beside him. He ran his hand up to her openness. That one hurt too; fragments of a life presumed dead. When would the light come. He would have to watch that pale cocaine edge pale like acetylene flame. And how could you dream of The Garden when what you would have had her have would have been a kind of beer fart: or, at best, the relief of a scarcely visible blackhead yielding to opposed thumbnails. Here it had been everything short of glacéed almonds and it made Skelton mean. When the shining city is at hand, a special slum will be built for me and my meanness. I will be the person, if that's what I am, in the slum; there will be one of everything; one rat, one tin can. The shining city will beckon in the distance. The shadow of the Bakunin monument will not quite stretch to my door. In the evening, the sound of happy syndicalist badminton finals will be borne to me on a sweet wind that sours as it enters my slum. I will behave poorly.

"Tom, what's the matter?"

"Jealousy."

"Well, that's wrong. And you weren't going to have any drugs any more."

"I wasn't going to have any jealousy any more either. You ought to see some of the things I wasn't going to have any more. I'd like to cold-shake about a teacupful of reds and fire them right now. I'm just sick with hurt and jealousy and going back on myself. I want some more of that coke. And then to have to hear a description of that Viennese organism. God."

Neither spoke for a time. Then Miranda said, "I'm twenty-four and I've been with a bunch of men—"

"—I know."

"For whom there was always at least affection."

"I understand."

"And I won't have it made an ugliness. You'll have to think of another kind of innocence. I've been trying to get through too, you know."

"I know, darling. I'm sorry. I want that of course too. But another thing comes in uh there, you see . . ."

They took the car and went to Rest Beach on the other side of the key. They could hear a fire engine down in the quarter off Simonton. It was hot and Skelton could smell fish in the garbage truck that went by bristling with palm leaves; a sign between the two men hanging off the back: WE CATER WEDDINGS. The wind was beginning to pull eastward into a weather change and the smell of City Electric was in the avenues.

They parked at Rest Beach and walked across between the sunbathers. There was not much wind and the sea was very plain under the empty sky. A long way off, a remote vessel, maybe a freighter, seemed absolutely still under its smoke which declined only slightly from the vertical before bluing away.

They walked out on the jetty, the sea trembling among the stones like gelatin. At the end, Miranda sat down, her brown thighs disappearing in her shorts. Her green, stony eyes did not seem to be seeing anything; and Skelton was not having a very good time.

"Haven't you ever walked in on a woman before?" Miranda asked, pushing her hair back over her ears with her thumbs.

"Yes."

"Once?"

"No, three times."

"And what were the women like?"

"They were types."

"They were all three types?"

"Two were types and one was a junkie."

"And what was I?"

"You were my girl."

Three striped sergeant-major fish, inches long, rested in the swell at their feet, surging in on each small roller, trusting the wave not to carry them clear to the rocks and riding out in it again, only to repeat in a loop, in and out again. The water was as green as the jar of squash blossoms.

"You look strange," said Miranda, "are you crashing from that cocaine?" Skelton said nothing. "Well, it's still Michael."

"I guess."

"Michael used to be my lover."

"Why do I have to be so stupid about this?"

"I don't know."

"I know better than to be this way."

"I know but you just are."

"I'll ride it out."

Though he knew he could still maintain, Skelton felt that voluminous hollow rush inside, that slippage of control systems, the cocaine express. Mild enough on the face of it, he had known it in other days to be the first step on the ride to the O.D. Corral. It was a family tradition to go the distance. This time it had to be in another quadrant because he had recently seen that tremulous threshold where another breath is a matter for decision.

"I was the victim of timing. I've been thinking about death all day. Don't ask me why. My mother told me this ungodly story—" Skelton at last could lose himself in something that would hold the jealousy away, stories of the dead, beginning with the man killed on the Indian mounds by bees; the usual powdered visages of cousins or acquaintances laid out next to an air conditioner or beneath a ceiling fan, more deeply foreign under their makeup than the maddest vices could have made them in life. Or when, in junior high, he had found with a friend a drowned Cuban nun in the cistern. No more than four and a half feet long she floated face down in the stagnant water, her habit flowing like wings amid clouds of immature frogs and mosquito larvae. When his friend's father, a pastry cook, came home, he looked into the cistern and said that he had known that she would do it sometime. Quite without passion, they carried the little body to the lawn; then all three at the same time dropped it on the grass, a black and white pile in draining cistern water and stranded tadpoles, a thing.

"That's dreadful."

"I know."

"Why did you tell me that?"

"There uh was some connection . . ."

"Between all this dead stuff and you walking in on me?"

"Yes!"

"Well, what was it," Miranda demanded.

"It's just that when you realize that everyone dies you become a terrible kind of purist. There just doesn't seem to be time for this other business."

"But darling that's all there is time for."

In the clear water at the jetty's end, the tide carried a few large jellyfish past. Ribbed as delicately as the squash blossoms, they swelled like a globe at the end of a glassblower's pipe; then pulsed suddenly in the direction of the tide.

"Let's get out of here."

THOMAS SKELTON THOUGHT THAT KEY WEST was a town he could only take so much of. Without the ocean, he knew he couldn't take it at all. It was one thing to be blanking out on a forty-hour week; and another to be unemployed and in Duval Street at a wrong hour; or in front of the Red Doors on Caroline Street when they came out with the stretcher and the shrimpers wandered into the night to smoke under the stars and look through the ambulance windows. The character with the knife was never cut off at the bar. He just strolled to the Wurlitzer and tried to remember exactly who he was. He played *The Orange Blossom Special* to someone down there looking at herself in the Formica who sat and never looked up. In the dreamboat evening of half-time wages the song was finished. The ambulance attendant held a hand mirror to the victim's mouth; and tried to remember if he mailed in the guarantee on his air conditioner. The shrimper's eyes filled to *The Orange Blossom Special*, which was his anthem. He recalled a childhood in Pascagoula when he'd never stabbed a soul, perforated a hymen, or put the boot to a man who was down.

Then too you could remember when you had been below Key West to the Marquesas on a cool winter day when the horsetails were on a rising barometer sky and the radiant drop curtain of fuchsia light stood on edge from the Gulf Stream. And when he ran back across the Boca Grande channel into the lakes and then toward Cottrell to miss the finger banks he knew how he would raise Key West on the soft-pencil edge of sea and sky. Then the city would seem like a white folding ruler, in sections; and the frame houses always lifted slowly, painted and wooden, from the sullen contours of the submarine base.

On the days when he was roughed up in the channel crossings and stopped for a drink to dry off, the up-country girl in a wash dress would offer him Seven Crown and Seven-up; so that the two of them could soar down Duval in a flood of artificial light, stars, and bugs.

Key West was a town where you had to pick and choose. It was always a favorite of pirates.

SKELTON WOULD NOT HAVE PICKED A FUSELAGE in a vacant lot next door to a rummy hotel if he had had a choice; but when the money ran out and half a dozen career daydreams collapsed like a telescope, those who might have helped failed to dart to his side. Impecunious as could be, his neighbors found his side trip into education rather fancy to begin with. House painting, culling shrimp, and the half-assed dream of being a guide had a homely recognizability. His popularity returned.

The fuselage, a remnant of a crash-landed navy reconnaissance plane, rested logically on a concrete form and had by now in the quick tropical growing seasons become impressively laced with strangler fig (a plant whose power was now slowly buckling the riveted aluminum panels), bougainvillea, Confederate star jasmine, and a delicate form of trumpeter vine whose blue translucent blossoms cascaded around the compression-sealed aerodynamic doorway.

Within the last month, an alcoholic drill sergeant had taken a room in the hotel; and every morning at seven o'clock, he drilled the winos in the back yard, the winos lurching across the packed earth under the early Key West sun, feet dragging in the dust and heads swinging under incomplete control on helpless and attenuated necks, hair slicked down, whitish blurred beards on some, veinous noses, broken teeth and bruises from falls. From his window in the morning, Skelton could only see the tops of their heads gliding and abruptly changing positions beyond the fence, the commands ringing out from the drill sergeant, the slow inexorable rise of absurd dust.

But today, coming home and closing the door, and opening his mind to the familiarity of his fuselage, Skelton felt a certain relief to be away from Carter and Dance, among whom he felt himself entirely to be the rube. Here in the fuselage, among Bohlke's *Fishes of the Bahamas, Field Notes on the Physiology of Marine Invertebrates*, and the entire Modern Library, from which, how many years ago, he had meant to assault the world on the most primal terms. Amid such familiarities, with all his ambitions flowing at once on parallel courses, it seemed to matter quite a lot less. He was a function of those continuities.

He dialed his mother's house.

"Mother, Tom. I can't make it for dinner; but I'll stop in sometime this evening. How's Dad?"

"He's resting nicely; if your grandpa would leave him be ..."

"Is he over there?"

"He came on the bike."

"How's Dad taking it?"

"Not so well, to tell the truth."

"Okay. I'll get by."

Skelton warmed some food from the Frigidaire: picadillo, fried plantains, yellow rice, black beans; making notes to himself on a pad. He ate and ruminated, the sound of commands coming through the fuselage window, the plaint of catbirds and the gentle flutter of vine and leaf touching the yielding air-stream contours of the fuselage. Skelton liked this place with its black anarchist flag, utilitarian bunk, desk, card table, propane stove, and Frigidaire. He could sit on top of the bunk by way of a Pullman ladder he had installed and look out among the tin roofs, the beautiful old shipwright houses, and the poinciana trees that grew with vivid mystery along his street. The cemetery was close enough that he could see from the foot of his street the bronze Victorian sailor, holding his oar, of the monument to the sailors of the *Maine;* and save for one house he could have seen across to the tennis courts and the statue of José Martí whose bust appeared that of a schoolboy in a false moustache, thumbing marble pages with a languorous hand; a memorial with some private character not lost in the inscription:

THE CUBAN LIBERTY APOSTLE

WISHED TO OFFER

TO THE PEOPLE OF KEY WEST

WHAT WAS LEFT OF HIS HEART

Nor in the graven homage of "Los Caballeros de la Luz," the horsemen of the light. Skelton could not see these things without some irrational desire to be a liberty apostle and horseman of the light, a shy delivery boy of eternity's loops.

A seabird-crowded sky made it quite impossible for Skelton to stay very long on land; and on the days when exaggerated tide fell below the mean low, exposing the flats around Key West and filling downwind side streets with the smell of ocean at its most fecund, he could grow quite frantic about it.

Today's revelations, the skiff and the bookings, he paid into his system slowly, having what he wanted.

He walked to his family's house on Peacon Lane; pulling the bell on the gate and waiting for his mother. She came without a word and let him through to the patio of old red street bricks. The deep bay porch swept out upon the patio in a watery-green cascade of vegetation and light, deep red pots of ferns hanging from the porch roof. At the far end of the patio, a small sprinkler turned and flung chains of glittering water up into the foliage-broken light; and high on the center of the green-floored porch was his father in his bed, covered by a gauzy mosquito canopy, his grandfather in a Cuban wicker chair beside.

"How are things?" he asked his mother.

"Fine."

"Mother, how are they?"

"Go over and talk to them."

"Evening, Grandpa."

"Tom."

"How're you feeling, Dad?"

"He feels perfectly well," volunteered the grandfather.

"If no one will get that asshole out of here," said the muted figure inside the gauze, "I will shit my pants and die on purpose."

"Do it!" said the grandfather. "You malinger well enough."

"*Grandpa.*"

"Every doctor in Key West says it is in his head—"

Mrs. Skelton was silent in the kitchen, an absentee ballot.

Skelton's father began to eat his pillow. Skelton reached gently under the canopy and pulled it from his tearing jaws; fluffs of eiderdown drifted on the porch.

"Someone run shit pig into the Gulf Stream," said Skelton's father. The grandfather stood and lashed into the gauze before Skelton forcibly seated him again.

"Go ahead," said the grandfather, drawing his glass of rum from under the chair. "Gang up."

"Come on now, Grandpa."

"Got a job yet, bright boy?"

"I'm starting."

"At what?"

"Guiding."

"Terrific. I'll see you at the Red Doors with the rest of the drunken charter-boat captains."

"I won't be at the Red Doors. And I'm skiff-guiding anyway. Also, when did you join the lecture tour?"

"Throw the old fart's ass over the wall," said Skelton's father.

"I'm hungry!" the old man bellowed toward the kitchen. Then in a hushed voice, "Look! Look! He's playing dead."

Skelton stood by the canopy. His father seemed to have passed. "Dad?"

"Let me go." A stertorous sigh issued from the youthful-looking man. He sat up suddenly and looked all about his familiar surroundings. "Piss."

"Not so easy there, is it now?" chuckled the grandfather.

Mrs. Skelton came to the door of the porch: "Soup's on!"

"What are we having?" the grandfather inquired.

"You'll like it."

"What are we having?"

"Jewfish chowder."

"I'm leaving. I can't eat that. I can't eat nigger food."

The grandfather went into the pantry and came out with a glass of water which he hurled through the canopy into the face of Skelton's father. "Life is beautiful!" he roared. "Can't you understand one thing? *Get out of bed!*"

Probably, seven months in bed had atrophied his muscles; so the grandfather's call for a Lazarus was a little fanciful. In any case, the often unpleasant old man hurried across the patio and out of the gate without another word. A whole section of the gauze was wet and clear. Inside, Skelton's father muttered with hatred a pastiche of maladroit quotations from Marlowe and local vulgarities.

Skelton was tasting the chowder, looking at chunks of jewfish and disks of carrots, parsnips, pieces of potato, onions, streaks of tomato turning and disappearing in the fragrant bisque with the turbulence of the wooden spoon he passed through the big pot. "I shouldn't have eaten," he said.

"The hell with that," said his mother. "You sit with him and talk."

Skelton deliberately sat next to the wet part of the canopy so that his father's features were as perceived in fog.

"Well, Dad."

"I like it this way, all right?"

"It seems like such a lot of trouble."

"All right, it seems like a lot of trouble."

"Grandpa out of sorts?"

"Your grandfather's Huey Long complex has finally put him beyond communication. I'm not sure the old bastard ever did have good sense." Skelton could see his father gesticulating emptily inside the canopy. "Aw, I take that back. But God he's wearing me out. If only he'd get old. But year after year, he wears us all out! It's inhuman!"

JAKE ROBERTS WAS ON THE DESK. "HELLO, Bubba," he said to Skelton. He called everyone Bubba. He sat next to the telephone and the teletype machine with which he had informationally ensnared various and sundry. He was always working on his "spread," by which he meant the variance between the cause of arrest and the eventual conviction based on teletype information. His best to date was an armed-robbery conviction arising from a loitering arrest. If he could get a murder conviction out of an unpaid parking ticket, jacking up the crime with teletype info, Jake would die happy. "Old boy has crossed his sef up," said the cyberneticist.

Skelton followed Roberts behind the desk to the holding room, whose cell held three tired shrimpers. "Let's make this official," said Roberts and scrawled a note on the pad on the fingerprinting desk. He put Skelton up to the height chart and photographed him with the Polaroid camera; then he unlocked the elevator with the key and on the way up handed Skelton his mug shot, with his height behind him, five feet eleven. They got out of the elevator on the second floor where you could look into the Greyhound station parking lot. Roberts left him at the first cell. Dance was there, all by himself.

"What do you want?" Dance asked, putting on the good cheer; he was not happy.

"Thought I'd check in and see if you needed anything."

"Nope."

"How you gettin on otherwise?"

"Real lousy. All my pigeons come home to roost."

"Well, it's not so bad." Skelton said. "Sure worked out for me. I haven't been able to get up cash money for a skiff."

"Well, now you have got you a skiff."

"Yes, sir!"

"And all them good bookings it took me ten years to cull out of all them bad bookings I didn't ask back."

"I do appreciate it."

"Well, we'll work something out."

"I understand that."

"There's only a hundred twenty hours on that engine. You should get a couple of years or more out of it." Dance grinned a little.

"Don't you think that's a little pessimistic about how long you're going to be in stir?"

"No, I don't," Nichol Dance said. "The dockmaster died." That was not so much a thing for Tom Skelton to think about as to receive like news of induction or perhaps curable carcinoma.

"It hardly seems you could have killed him."

"I didn't. I just popped that little hole in him and he leaked out and quit. I feel like I been framed."

"I can't think what to say."

"Oh for God's sake! Go on now. Visit me another time."

Skelton started away. Nichol Dance called to him.

"About that other," he called, "we'll work something out."

"Mutual aid," said Skelton, in honor of his father.

WALKING FROM THE FOOT OF WILLIAM TO THE foot of Margaret, among all the shrimp boats driven in by heavy weather, some with the net spilled in one place on the deck and others with the net streaming gauzily from the boom, various sea animals stranded in the web, Tom Skelton thinks: Of all my idiocies this one of guiding is the silliest; no it is not.

You could, he decided, erode everything always with these inquiries as to higher meaning. Now let us think of something amusing. From a single mustard seed grew a gargling violin. Why did the moron tiptoe past the medicine cabinet. Hm. Around the bases of the piers the green water was racing and whitening, racing back under his feet and colliding resonantly in the under-pier darkness.

James Davis, a slender gaunt gesticulatory fellow with walnut-shaped eyes and a face the color of birch stain, was skipper of the shrimper *Marquesa*. In years past he was the boon companion and, in some spiritual sense, the underling cohort of Skelton's father.

James Davis and Tom Skelton sat together in the wheelhouse of the *Marquesa*, James with his feet on the chart desk, looking up out of one window in recollection, himself partly obscured to Skelton's view in the shadows of navigational and depth-finding electronics.

". . . when your old man came of draft age, he would talk about shooting away his big toe or going to Cuba for a dose. Then Uncle called him up and he went to Fort Benning for basic but returned in real short order."

Returned, Skelton knew, discharged as insane after a corps of officers met to determine just what would hamstring him longer in civilian life than a dishonorable discharge. In healthy quarters even then, a dishonorable discharge was no more than a certificate of some racy proclivity. But insane made folks jumpy.

Racy proclivities he had had even in the years Skelton's grandfather was in the state senate fabricating remunerative franchises around the state and establishing a gerrymandered kingdom for himself that in the face of subsequent investigations at the federal level proved to have nine lives; in countless Gulf Coast communities Skelton's grandfather was revered unseen and unmet as only a crook of limitless cynicism can be revered. Ultimately, various congeries of "Miami Jews and legal swindlers out of the District of Columbia," later replaced by simple "Castro sympathizers," nibbled old man Skelton's duchy to that small country below Big Pine. Here he retrenched, bilking everything and everyone when money changed hands, being downright fatherly about it, right up to the point he suggested a divvy on the city-wide bolita games; at which time a cadre of "Castro types" arranged to have half his ass blown away with the time-honored, sawed-off shotgun. Murder was intended, and before anyone could try again, the old man let up on the bolita. The true residue of this incident was another myth of old man Skelton hightailing it behind the Fourth of July restaurant, flat out as a sprinter, the shotgun barking in the humid night and driving his own self to Monroe General with half his backside still in the street.

". . . your dad meantime was trying to go straight listening to his classical music on the victrola. But with that father of his, he couldn't help himself: he run some guns to Cuba; he horsewhipped the navy-base commander for calling up his girlfriend; he fished with me; he studied all the time for no good reason and went out to drink himself crazy five nights a week . . ."

"Was this girlfriend my mother?"

"Yes, it was."

"Tell me what she was like."

"I'm always telling you that. I'll tell you another time . . ." Skelton never got an answer to this question.

They sat in the wheelhouse, neither of them fishing because of the blow that made the rigging clatter overhead.

"What have you got for power in this thing?" Skelton asked. To him, shop talk was always lyric.

"Detroit Diesels with Capitol reverse and reduction gears and a Lister auxiliary."

"It's a Lantana."

"No sir, a Desco, out of St. Augustine. I bought it off of David Rawlin's widow the year he died. It needed work."

"Do you know this flats guide, Nichol Dance?"

"Heard of him."

"He killed a man yesterday."

James looked out at the scudding clouds. "No doubt," he said.

SKELTON, HIKING TO THE DOCK, THOUGHT about Nichol Dance. In Skelton's mind, Nichol Dance was saying again, "About that other, we'll work something out." The imprecision of the remark troubled Skelton.

It was that like so many of us Skelton had tried quite hard not to be crazy. Largely lucid and more than normally unaddled by abstract ambitions, Skelton had from time to time lapsed curiously into not terribly human actions. Perhaps it was his sense of humor; but, well, anyway he seems to have done some barking.

At first, it was inadvertent; or, as a joke. Then, once, he had driven back the urge to bark as though it were the embodiment of terror: to wit, that he was not human at all and that one day he would find himself beside a half-filled garbage pail, baying at the moon.

"You are baying at the moon now," said a face once from the speeding Lagonda. "Right now."

"WELL SIR," SAID CARTER, STACKING THE FRO-zen balao in one end of the bait freezer, "it sorely grieves me to think of the mess he is in. But I would say that in view of his record, Nichol is all through." But then, Carter was smiling.

"It doesn't seem fair," said Skelton.

"Oh sure it's fair. I mean, Nichol is a good friend. But honestly, you don't jump up and gaff folks."

"I suppose—"

"You suppose?"

"I mean, I suppose you don't."

A few minutes later, Carter said, "What was that?"

"What?"

"I heard barking."

JAKE ROBERTS GAVE SKELTON THE ELEVATOR KEY and said, "They got him for the whole thing, hook, line, and sinker." Jake was grinning too.

Nichol Dance was asleep. "Nichol?"

"Why, the keed," said Dance, getting up readily and coming to the front of the cell. "Have you heard the news?"

"I believe so."

"I'm going to use my connections to get on a road gang."

Skelton didn't know whether he was to laugh or not.

"Are you . . . worried?" Nichol Dance didn't look worried.

"Hell yes I'm worried. About a lot of things. Not the least of which is my next piece of tail is in twenty years. That actually hurts my feelings. I'm the kind of person would fuck a brush pile if I thought they was a snake in it. —What are you laughing at?"

"Nothing."

"Did you ever hear of Charlie Starkweather?"

"Yes."

"Charlie Starkweather is what happens when you push someone around once too often. They laughed at him when he stuttered. They called him a redheaded bowlegged woodpecker. Starkweather used to wear Tony Lama boots. He used to hang out in used-clothing stores. He wanted to marry a cocktail hostess and set-tle—you know—*down*. He killed eleven people outside of Lincoln, Nebraska, and owned a '49 Merc chopped and channeled with a bullnosed hood and frenched headlights."

"What does the '49 Merc have to do with the eleven people?" Skelton said, confused.

"It's just part of the whole story, is all. Charlie Starkweather was sort of an artist. He used to draw pictures of himself committing the killings. It appeared like he was spraying them people with a garden hose and they was just all folded up around the bullets . . ."

"That's kind of . . . different."

"Well, it was extreme of him. But his life was real colorful. I have one thing against him though: he had no sense of humor. You should never kill somebody if it isn't funny."

"I don't like that idea."

"That's because you don't understand it."

"I suppose. But anyway Nichol, I wanted to get by before you headed for Raiford and uh well at least thank you for letting me take the boat while you're away."

"Oh, glad to do it, glad to do it." He had one hand in his pocket and hung by the other from one of the vertical bars. "We'll work something out. And tell Jake, would you, I want a salad tonight."

THE WEATHER BROKE, STREAMED AWAY IN mackerel clouds, cleared and got hot. He would guide in the morning. He was on Duval Street now. The Conch Train drifted past Sloppy Joe's and a thousand screaming ninnies cheered the clanging bell the barmaid rang at them as they passed. In the window of Gomez Plumbing the Christmas display rested on a field of palm leaves: Mary, Joseph, and Christ in His manger, entirely fabricated from plumbing parts; the head of Holy Mary Mother of God was a squat chromium faucet; the Christ Child was a lovingly assembled congestion of pipe fittings in a cardboard manger. A simple faith, thought Skelton unkindly, but it is mine.

He had a bowl of *fabada asturiana* at the Cacique and then a double Jim Beam across the street at the Anchor. There were foreign sailors leapfrogging down Duval Street, squealing and blocking traffic, until a huge black police lieutenant scattered them among the side streets. The sun went down and the light came up on the side of the La Concha Hotel.

Skelton wandered over to Eaton and sat on one of the benches donated by Mayor Papy, smoked a Canary Island cigar, waved to people he knew, and worried about guiding. He thumbed open Nichol Dance's date-book: "Mr. and Mrs. Robert Rudleigh, Rumson, Connecticut." Well.

Skelton tried quite earnestly to think about Mr. and Mrs. Robert Rudleigh of Rumson, Connecticut. He imagined a brick house where Revolutionary War soldiers had fired at the British, a house with grapeshot in the lintels, covered with vines, and into whose front door Mr. Robert Rudleigh went each winter's dusk, carrying an enormous newspaper and wearing a gray coat. "Darling," he would have said to Mrs. Rudleigh, "it is time we had sport." Then the Rudleighs go to the city of New York. They go to a great brown store where pictures of Theodore Roosevelt and stuffed heads of tigers adorn the walls. A well-mannered lesbian shows them "tropical outfits" which include mosquito netting, a bonefish rod, a pith helmet, and a prophylactic; all stapled to a large piece of cardboard upon which has been printed a "tropical scene," the entire outfit protected by cellophane and displayed under a disinfecting ultraviolet light. Rudleigh's motto is, "I pay, I take." The city of New York and the town of Rumson know him for what he is: a marvel in a gray coat who sometimes walks chest deep through snowdrifts to get that enormous newspaper; and who only occasionally breaks a savage work pattern for sport in the tropics.

He pulled the bell on the gate, now locked, as it was not in his childhood; now barbed wire was stapled along the top of the wooden wall. As a child, he sat in the uncultivated end of the enclosed lot and listened to the chameleons rattling in the deep grass, crawled low in that grass and watched the lizards leap out green and tremulous into the streaked sunlight.

Lying on his back he had watched a spider let itself down forty feet from the Alexandria palm inch by inch over a period of hours; so that after watching until it had magnified to subsume the world, the sky itself seemed to radiate from its back. The spider, noxiously banana-shaped, landed on his face, walked away and thus vanished.

"Come in and leave that cigar in the driveway."

"Can't stop but a minute. I just wanted to say hi."

He walked over to the gauze canopy.

"Evening, Dad."

"Tom."

"What are you doing?"

"Reading Shakespeare."

Skelton had come to associate the higher arts with his father's holing up in bed.

"I also have my violin in here," he added.

Skelton could barely see inside; but after an instant's rustling about, a phrase from Sibelius flowed out through the gauze; then, imperceptibly blurred into Hank Williams's *Lovesick Blues*. Skelton listened to those abject hillbilly strains a long moment, remembering his father on the porch in his Cuban chair so many years ago now, playing for his pals, fishermen, idlers, and crazies. The music stopped.

"MA'AM, YOU WANT TO HAND ME THAT LUNCH so I can stow it?" Skelton took the wicker basket from Mrs. Rudleigh; and then the thermos she handed him. "I've got plenty of water," he said.

"That's not water."

"What is it?"

"Gibsons."

"Let me put them in the cooler for you then—"

"We put them in the thermos," said Rudleigh, "so we don't have to put them in the cooler. We like them where we can get at them. In case we need them, you know, real snappy."

Tom Skelton looked up at him. Most people when they smile expose a section of their upper teeth; when Rudleigh smiled, he exposed his lower teeth.

"Hold the thermos in your lap," Skelton said. "If that starts rolling around the skiff while I'm running these banks, I'll throw it overboard."

"An ecologist," said Mrs. Rudleigh.

"Are you sure Nichol cannot appeal his sentence, Captain?" asked Rudleigh.

"I'm sure," said Skelton.

Mrs. Rudleigh reached out one hand and bent it backward so her fingernails were all in display; she was thinking of a killer line but it wouldn't come; so she didn't speak.

Skelton knew from other guides he could not let the clients run the boat for him; but he had never expected this; now all three of them were glancing past one another with metallic eyes.

Mrs. Rudleigh came and Skelton put her in the forward chair. Rudleigh followed in squeaking bright deck shoes and sat aft, swiveling about in the chair with an executive's preoccupation.

"Captain," Rudleigh began. Men like Rudleigh believed in giving credit to the qualified. If an eight-year-old were running the skiff, Rudleigh would call him "Captain" without irony; it was a credit to his class. "Captain, are we going to bonefish?" Mrs. Rudleigh was putting zinc oxide on her thin nose and on the actual edges of her precise cheekbones. She was a thin pretty woman of forty who you could see had a proclivity for hysterics, slow burns, and slapping.

"We have a good tide for bonefish."

"Well, Missus Rudleigh and I have had a good deal

of bonefishing in Yucatán and we were wondering if it mightn't be an awfully long shot to fish for permit . . ."

Skelton knew it was being put to him; finding permit—big pompano—was a guide's hallmark and he didn't particularly have a permit tide. "I can find permit," he said though, finishing a sequence Rudleigh started with the word "Captain."

Carter strolled up. He knew the Rudleighs and they greeted each other. "You're in good hands," he said to them, tilting his head toward Skelton. "Boy's a regular fish hawk." He returned his head to the perpendicular.

"Where are your people, Cart?" Skelton asked to change the subject.

"They been partying, I guess. Man said he'd be late. Shortens my day."

Skelton choked the engine and started it. He let it idle for a few minutes and then freed up his lines. The canal leading away from the dock wandered around lazily, a lead-green gloss like pavement.

"Ought to find some bonefish in the Snipes on this incoming water," Carter said. Skelton looked at him a moment.

"We're permit fishing, Cart."

"Oh, really. Why, permit huh."

"What do you think? Boca Chica beach?"

"Your guess is as good as mine. But yeah okay, Boca Chica."

Skelton idled on the green tidal gloss of the canal until he cleared the entrance, then ran it up to 5,000 rpm and slacked off to an easy plane in the light chop. He leaned back over his shoulder to talk to Rudleigh. "We're going to Boca Chica beach. I think it's our best bet for permit on this tide."

"Fine, fine."

"I hate to take you there, a little bit, because it's in the landing pattern."

"I don't mind if the fish don't mind."

Skelton swung in around by Cow Key channel, past the navy hospital, under the bridge where boys were getting in some snapper fishing before it would be time for the military hospitals; then out the channel along the mangroves with the great white wing of the drive-in theater to their left, with an unattended meadow of loudspeaker stanchions; and abruptly around the corner to an expanse of blue Atlantic. Skelton ran tight to the beach, inside the boat-wrecking niggerheads; he watched for sunken ice cans and made the run to Boca Chica, stopping short.

The day was clear and bright except for one squall to the west, black with etched rain lines connecting it to sea; the great reciprocating engine of earth, thought Skelton, looks like a jellyfish.

"Go ahead and get ready, Mr. Rudleigh, I'm going to pole us along the rocky edge and see what we can see." Skelton pulled the pushpole out of its chocks and got up in the bow; Rudleigh was ready in the stern behind the tilted engine. It took two or three leaning thrusts to get the skiff underway; and then they were gliding over the sand, coral, sea fans, staghorn, and lawns of turtle grass. Small cowfish, sprats, and fry of one description or another scattered before them and vanished in the glare. Stone crabs backed away in bellicose, Pentagonian idiocy in the face of the boat's progress. Skelton held the boat into the tide at the breaking edge of the flat and looked for moving fish.

A few small sharks came early on the flood and passed down light, yellow-eyed and sweeping back and forth schematically for something in trouble. The first military aircraft came in overhead, terrifyingly low; a great delta-winged machine with howling, vulvate exhausts and nervous quick-moving control flaps; so close were they that the bright hydraulic shafts behind the flaps glittered; small rockets were laid up thickly under the wings like insect eggs. The plane approached, banked subtly, and the pilot glanced out at the skiff; his head looking no larger than a cocktail onion. A moment after the plane passed, its shock wave swept toward them and the crystal, perfect world of the flat paled and vanished; not reappearing until some minutes later and slowly. The draconic roar of the engines diminished and twin blossoms of flame shrank away toward the airfield.

"It must take a smart cookie," said Mrs. Rudleigh, "to make one of those do what it is supposed to."

"It takes balls for brains," said Rudleigh.

"That's even better," she smiled.

"Only that's what any mule has," Rudleigh added.

Mrs. Rudleigh threw something at her husband, who remained in the stern, rigid as a gun carriage.

Skelton was so determined that this first day of his professional guiding be a success that he felt with some agony the ugliness of the aircraft that came in now at shorter and shorter intervals, thundering with their volatile mists drifting over the sea meadow.

The Rudleighs had opened the thermos and were consuming its contents exactly as the heat of the day began to spread. Skelton was now poling down light, flushing small fish; then two schools of bonefish, not tailing but pushing wakes in their hurry; Rudleigh saw them late and bungled the cast, looking significantly at Mrs. Rudleigh after each failure.

"You've got to bear down," she said.

"I'm bearing down."

"Bear down harder, honey."

"I said: I'm bearing down."

Now the wading birds that were on the flat in the early tide were flooded out and flew northwest to catch the Gulf of Mexico tide. Skelton knew they had about lost their water.

"It's kind of slow, Captain," said Rudleigh.

"I've been thinking the same thing," Skelton said, his heart chilling within him. "I'm going to pole this out and make a move."

A minute later, he was running to Saddlebunch and got there in time to catch the incoming water across the big sand spot; he hardly had a moment to stake the skiff when the bonefish started crossing the sand. Now Mrs. Rudleigh was casting, driving the fish away. Rudleigh snatched the rod from her after her second failure.

"*Sit down!*"

Rudleigh was rigidly prepared for the next fish. Skelton would have helped him but knew in advance it would make things worse. He felt all of his efforts pitted against the contents of the thermos.

"You hawse's oss," said Mrs. Rudleigh to her husband. He seemed not to have heard. He was in the vague crouch of lumbar distress.

"I can fish circles around you, queen bee," he said after a bit. "Always could."

"What about Peru? What about Cabo Blanco?"

"You're always throwing Cabo Blanco in my face without ever, repeat, ever a word about Tierra del Fuego."

"What about Piñas Bay, Panama."

"Shut up."

"Seems to me," she said, "that Raúl commented that the señora had a way of making the señor look real bum."

A small single bonefish passed the skiff. Rudleigh flushed it by casting right into its face. "*Cocksucker.*"

"That's just the way you handled striped marlin. Right there is about what you did with those stripes at Rancho Buena Vista."

Rudleigh whirled around and held the point of his rod under Mrs. Rudleigh's throat. "*I'm warning you.*"

"He had a tantrum at the Pez Maya Club in Yucatán," Mrs. Rudleigh told Skelton.

"Yes, ma'am. I see."

"*Uh, Captain—*"

"I'm right here, Mr. Rudleigh."

"I thought this was a permit deal."

"I'm looking for permit on this tide. I told you they were a long shot."

"Captain, I know about permit. I have seen permit in the Bahamas, Yucatán, Costa Rica, and at the great Belize camps in British Honduras. I know they are a long shot."

Skelton said, "Maybe your terrific familiarity with places to fish will tell us where we ought to be right now."

"Captain, I wouldn't presume."

A skiff was running just off the reef, making sheets of bright water against the sun.

"Do you know what today's tides are?" Skelton asked.

"No."

"Which way is the Gulf of Mexico?"

Rudleigh pointed all wrong. Skelton wanted to be home reading Proudhon, studying the winos, or copulating.

"Is that a permit?" Mrs. Rudleigh asked. The black fork of a large permit surfaced just out of casting range: beyond belief. Rudleigh stampeded back into position.

Skelton slipped the pole out of the sand and began to ghost quietly toward the fish and stopped. Nothing visible. A long moment passed. Again, the black fork appeared.

"Cast."

Rudleigh threw forty feet beyond the permit. There was no hope of retrieving and casting again. Then out of totally undeserved luck, the fish began to change course toward Rudleigh's bait. Rudleigh and Mrs. Rudleigh exchanged glances.

"Please keep your eye on the fish." Skelton was overwhelmed by the entirely undeserved nature of what was transpiring. In a moment, the big fish was tailing again.

"Strike him."

Rudleigh lifted the rod and the fish was on. Skelton poled hard, following the fish, now streaking against the drag for deep water. The same skiff that passed earlier appeared, running the other direction; and Skelton wondered who it could be.

"God, Captain, will I be able to cope with this at all? I mean, I knew the fish was strong! But honest to God, this is a nigger with a hotfoot!"

"I'm still admiring your cast, darling."

Skelton followed watching the drawn bow the rod had become, the line shearing water with precision.

"What a marvelously smooth drag this reel has! A hundred smackers seemed steep at the time; but when you're in the breach, as I am now, a drag like this is the last nickel bargain in America!"

Skelton was poling after the fish with precisely everything he had. And it was difficult on the packed bottom with the pole inclining to slip out from under him.

His feeling of hope for a successful first-day guiding

was considerably modified by Rudleigh's largely un-deserved hooking of the fish. And now the nobility of the fish's fight was further eroding Skelton's pleasure.

When they crossed the edge of the flat, the permit raced down the reef line in sharp powerful curves, drag-ging the line across the coral. "Gawd, gawd, gawd," Rudleigh said. "This cookie is stronger than I am!" Skelton poled harder and at one point overtook the fish as it desperately rubbed the hook on the coral bottom; seeing the boat, it flushed once more in terror, making a single long howl pour from the reel. A fish that was exactly noble, thought Skelton, who began to imagine the permit coming out of a deep-water wreck by the pull of moon and tide, riding the invisible crest of the in-coming water, feeding and moving by force of blood; only to run afoul of an asshole from Connecticut.

The fight continued without much change for an-other hour, mainly outside the reef line in the green water over a sand bottom: a safe place to fight the fish. Rudleigh had soaked through his khaki safari clothes; and from time to time Mrs. Rudleigh advised him to "bear down." When Mrs. Rudleigh told him this, he would turn to look at her, his neck muscles standing out like cords and his eyes acquiring broad white perime-ters. Skelton ached from pursuing the fish with the pole; he might have started the engine outside the reef line, but he feared Rudleigh getting his line in the propeller and he had found that a large fish was held away from the boat by the sound of a running engine.

As soon as the fish began to show signs of tiring, Skelton asked Mrs. Rudleigh to take a seat; then he brought the big net up on the deck beside him. He hoped he would be able to get Rudleigh to release this hugely undeserved fish, not only because it was unde-served but because the fish had fought so very bravely.

No, he admitted to himself, Rudleigh would never let the fish go.

By now the fish should have been on its side. It began another long and accelerating run, the pale sheet of water traveling higher up the line, the fish swerving somewhat inshore again; and to his terror, Skelton found himself poling after the fish through the shallows, now and then leaning over to free the line from a sea fan. They glided among the little hammocks and mangrove keys of Saddlebunch in increasing vegetated congestion, in a narrowing tidal creek that closed around and over them with guano-covered mangroves and finally prevented the boat from following another foot. Nevertheless, line continued to pour off the reel.

"Captain, consider it absolutely necessary that I kill the fish. This one doubles the Honduran average."

Skelton did not reply, he watched the line slow its passage from the reel, winding out into the shadowy creek; then stop. He knew there was a good chance the desperate animal had reached a dead end.

"Stay here."

Skelton climbed out of the boat and, running the line through his fingers lightly, began to wade the tidal creek. The mosquitoes found him quickly and held in a pale globe around his head. He waded steadily, flushing herons out of the mangroves over his head. At one point, he passed a tiny side channel, blocking the exit of a heron that raised its stiff wings very slightly away from its body and glared at him. In the green shadows, the heron was a radiant, perfect white.

He stopped a moment to look at the bird. All he could hear was the slow musical passage of tide in the mangrove roots and the low pattern of bird sounds more liquid than the sea itself in these shallows. He moved away from the side channel, still following the line. Occasionally, he felt some small movement of life in it; but he was certain now the permit could go no farther. He had another thirty yards to go, if he had guessed right looking at Rudleigh's partially emptied spool.

Wading along, he felt he was descending into the permit's world; in knee-deep water, the small mangrove snappers, angelfish, and baby barracudas scattered before him, precise, contained creatures of perfect mobility. The brilliant blue sky was reduced to a narrow ragged band quite high overhead now and the light wavered more with the color of the sea and of estuarine shadow than that of vulgar sky. Skelton stopped and his eye followed the line back in the direction he had come. The Rudleighs were at its other end, infinitely far away.

Skelton was trying to keep his mind on the job he had set out to do. The problem was, he told himself, to go from Point A to Point B; but every breath of humid air, half sea, and the steady tidal drain through root and elliptical shadow in his ears and eyes diffused his attention. Each heron that leaped like an arrow out of his narrow slot, spiraling invisibly into the sky, separated him from the job. Shafts of light in the side channels illuminated columns of pristine, dancing insects.

Very close now. He released the line so that if his appearance at the dead end terrified the permit there would not be sufficient tension for the line to break. The sides of the mangrove slot began to yield. Skelton stopped.

An embowered, crystalline tidal pool: the fish lay exhausted in its still water, lolling slightly and unable to right itself. It cast a delicate circular shadow on the sand bottom. Skelton moved in and the permit made no effort to rescue itself; instead, it lay nearly on its side and watched Skelton approach with a steady, following eye that was, for Skelton, the last straw. Over its broad, virginal sides a lambent, moony light shimmered. The fish seemed like an oval section of sky—yet sentient and alert, intelligent as tide.

He took the permit firmly by the base of its tail and turned it gently upright in the water. He reached into its mouth and removed the hook from the cartilaginous operculum. He noticed that the suddenly loosened line was not retrieved: Rudleigh hadn't even the sense to keep tension on the line.

By holding one hand under the permit's pectoral fins and the other around the base of its tail, Skelton was able to move the fish back and forth in the water to revive it. When he first tentatively released it, it teetered over on its side, its wandering eye still fixed upon him. He righted the fish again and continued to move it gently back and forth in the water; and this time when he released the permit, it stayed upright, steadying itself in equipoise, mirror sides once again purely reflecting the bottom. Skelton watched a long while until some regularity returned to the movement of its gills.

Then he cautiously—for fear of startling the fish—backed once more into the green tidal slot and turned to head for the skiff. Rudleigh had lost his permit.

The line was lying limp on the bottom. Why didn't the fool at least retrieve it? With this irritation, Skelton began to return to normal. He trudged along the creek, this time against the tide; and returned to the skiff.

The skiff was empty.

THE SEARCH FOR THE RUDLEIGHS WAS LONG and exhausting. The only thing Tom Skelton could imagine was that they had gone wading for shells and been caught by the tide among the mangroves, unable to return to the skiff. Because of the variation in depths, he could not use the engine and had instead to continue poling among the little keys. His search was very thorough; and when he had finished with it, he was no longer able to imagine that the tide had caught them shelling. His mind began to cling to a sequence of horrific conjectures . . . water-swollen bodies tangled in the stems of brain corals, for instance; Ma and Pa Rudleigh goggling in Davey Jones's locker.

The sun was starting down; and to the west he could see the navy aircraft landing lights in the dusk. He simply could not think of another thing to do. He decided to return to the dock and contact the Coast Guard. He started the engine and ran toward Key West. The military aircraft were coming in with regularity, their lights streaming.

His hands were blistered, and hurt against the steering wheel. He quartered, down sea, running wide open, and the boat twisted sharply when the forefoot dug, twisting the wheel against his blistered hands.

Skelton landed the boat and tied it quickly; it was the end of his first day of professional guiding. He had no trophies to send to the taxidermist in Miami; he had lost both the fish and his clients.

He ran inside the bait shack. Myron Moorhen, the accountant, was sitting at the desk poring over long yellow sheets under a gooseneck lamp. "Cart said you was to come across the street soon as you came in. He's in the lounge."

"I've got a problem—"

"That's what it's about."

Skelton looked at him for a long moment, then headed for Roosevelt Boulevard. It was a warm night, ready for rain, and the headlights on the street streamed a wet, lactic yellow while he waited to cross. He ran between cars, hearing sudden brakes, and ran into the entryway of the Sandpiper Lounge, stopping in the air-conditioned near-darkness to get his bearings.

The bar was in front of him, five rows of bottles against a mirror with a fluorescent light over them; and perhaps a dozen people at the bar. Beyond the bar were the rest rooms, marked with the profile of a ballerina on one, a top hat and cane on the other. Johnny Mathis sang from the jukebox, sounding as if he'd swallowed an intra-uterine coil.

Out of the men's room stepped Nichol Dance. He walked not very steadily to the bar and joined Cart, the Rudleighs, and Roy the dockmaster, whose bandages bulged his already enormous midriff.

Tom Skelton began to track back through his mind. He remembered the skiff passing in two directions off the reef line that afternoon. It would have been Cart and Nichol; he remembered back in the mangroves, on Nichol's fortieth suicide attempt, that talk about their overcrowded profession, only now, he realized, directed at him. Roy the dockmaster never died and Nichol never went to Raiford; and Tom Skelton was evidently no longer a guide.

Rudleigh spotted him standing in the doorway and saluted him with a cocktail.

Skelton turned quickly out of sight into the entryway, leaned against the cigarette machine a moment looking out onto the boulevard. It was dark and the rain had thrown a huge corolla around the moon. Skelton's mind had just locked and was letting the finest thin stream of information in, a little at a time. Over the low crown of hill in the gleaming road, the smeared yellow lights mounted and dropped toward him out of a canyon of useless small businesses and franchised outrages.

When you were down and out in Hotcakesland, there were always monuments of smut upon which to rest the mind. He looked at his hands.

The heat burned up his neck and into his brain. A cocktail hostess late for work ran past in a wet raincoat, the wet heat of the night darting in against processed air. Then from the kitchen a figure passed, blurred underneath a tray of bright trembling jellies. Suddenly, Skelton's brain began to fill with violence. He calmed himself, leaned over and touched fingers to the buttons of the cigarette machine, Kools, Luckies, Silva thins, Marlboros; and considered.

This time, crossing, he had all the patience in the world for a clearing in the traffic. The rain came light and warm and vertical in windless air equally upon Skelton and upon the ocean and upon the boats along the Bight brightening under its fall. The corrugated roofs of the equipment sheds looked shining and combed; and the sky was translucent enough for the broad, watery moon to show through.

Myron Moorhen the accountant could still be seen through the window of the bait shack, scratching at a yellow sheet and running his fingers deep into his hair. "I've got a problem," Skelton had said. "That's what it's about," he said, bored but part of the joke.

To be a fool. A fool in one of Skelton's children's books had had a red, V-shaped mouth.

Skelton eased himself over the side of the dock next to the skiff into the warm water. Some phosphor glowed at his movement. He untied the skiff's lines.

When Skelton's father took to his bed, Skelton's grandfather raged through the house looking for something bad enough to say; all he could come up with was the accusation that Skelton's father was no fool. From afar, his father could be heard in healthy laughter; then, accompanying himself on the violin:

> "*I'm an old cow hand,*
> *Not an old cow foot . . .*"

And the grandfather raging in to smash the violin and Skelton's father holding him by the throat, shutting off his wind and asking with utmost loathing and mania, "Wouldn't someone drop Mister Pig Shit in the Gulf Stream for me?"

Now easing the skiff away from its mooring and listening for movement on the dock, Skelton could sometimes touch bottom, sometimes only tread water. He had a thirty-yard stretch of canal flooded by the security light next to the bait shack and when he cleared that he would be safe. A door opened and closed in the shack: Moorhen wandering out still staring at his yellow sheets. He headed across the street to the lounge. Skelton began to rush, to push with all he had, and to rush.

Darkness: a basin in the canal, the gentle pull of running tide, the moon overhead trying to drag him to sea. Merle Haggard says every fool has a rainbow. I am safe here. Skelton climbed aboard and looked back out of his bay of darkness. The boulevard was a lighted stage, cars entering and exiting in opposite directions. The lounge was upstage center; on its roof an enormous profile of a sandpiper, outlined in neon and ungodly in the mercury-vapor light from the street. Hotcakesland. It is all for sale, thought Skelton.

He pulled the fuel line out from under the gunwale, and cut it; then rocked the boat so the surge in the tank would force fuel onto the deck. Gasoline was quickly everywhere.

Skelton sat down to rest and wait for all the gas to flow. He opened the small dunnage box by the controls and took out a book of matches that read, he strangely noticed, *Hands tied because you lack a high school diploma?;* then the rag with which he had wiped down the deck when he refueled the skiff.

Out of the lounge, pausing momentarily beneath the neon beak of the sandpiper while traffic cleared, came the Rudleighs, Carter, Nichol Dance, Roy the dockmaster, and Myron Moorhen the accountant. Skelton looked at them. A moment earlier they had streamed out of the land of frozen daiquiris, past a buffet table covered with molded fruit medleys, past the fifteen chromium selector levers of the cigarette machine, and into the cloacal American night. Skelton on his lunar, fetid inshore tide did not for the moment belong to the nation; except in the sense that the two principal questions of citizenship, *Will-I-be-caught?* and *Can-I-get-away?*, dominated his mind entirely, only slightly modified by the prime New World lunacy of getting from Point A to Point B.

They were moving toward the dock, all facing forward rather than toward each other, which was strange: the Rudleighs were customers, and when you are around customers, you point your face at them. You are selling and they are buying.

Skelton was out of the skiff once more, matches in his mouth, oily rag in hand. He treaded water away from the skiff, keeping the rag high in the air; then he held himself in position, lit the balled-up rag, tossed it into the boat.

Flame zigzagged up and down the boat's interior with a sucking noise until the entire thing was afire. Low in the water and swimming through darkness toward the far side of the basin, Skelton could no longer see the five people crossing the street. Then suddenly they popped up on the dock. Carter and Dance boarded Carter's skiff and the engine started with a roar. They jumped the skiff up to planing speed, then shut down abruptly as Nichol Dance's skiff coughed into explosion, a ball of flame blowing flat out sideways through the hull, then up like liquid into the sky, pieces of the hull soaring up in the fountain, one piece sailing like a comet over the joyous face of Skelton, trailing flame and fire. Then the boat sank so abruptly that Carter and Dance vanished in the darkness like Skelton.

Skelton listened to the engine. The skiff rose up against the light of the boulevard, Carter at the wheel, Dance in the bow with a gun. Skelton didn't move.

The skiff traveled in a slow curve and vanished in the darkness between Skelton and the shore. The dim moon overhead and Skelton's lowness in the water kept him from seeing.

The skiff appeared once more against the light, very slowly; then modified its course in the narrow quarters so that Skelton could see they would find him if he did not think of something.

The skiff was coming toward him. He would submerge; but the boat was moving so very slowly that he would have to stay down for a good while; he had to judge the last minute. The skiff kept coming and at a range of fifty feet, the skiff against the light, Skelton submerged and gripped deeply into the bottom thinking giddily that if he grabbed an eel or sting ray he would have to hang on to it. He could hear the engine very well down here; and in a moment the skiff was overhead. Skelton looked up and saw the pearly trail from the engine, the skiff soaring against the moon, the shadow of Nichol Dance wavering past. Skelton's blood lagged in his brain.

The engine sang by. Skelton stayed on the bottom until he could bear to no longer and then surfaced. The skiff was transom toward him, heading for the dock, the water mercurial and brilliant in the security light.

The Rudleighs—no one knew why—were slapping each other on the dock. The surprise of that helped guarantee Skelton's life. The two guides jumped ashore and separated them. Mrs. Rudleigh spat; her husband's hat was askew.

Meanwhile, Skelton was suffering spiritually what is known on commercial aircraft as "a sudden loss of cabin pressure"; and his discovery of the Rudleigh's combat was like the dropping of the emergency oxygen mask into his lap. So he convinced himself that he was safe, forever really.

THOMAS SKELTON, WHOSE AIM HAD BEEN TO be a practicing Christian, was now a little gone in the faith. But, he thought, no matter; and took some comfort to remember the Gospel according to St. Matthew: *Whosoever shall say, Thou fool, shall be in danger of hell-fire.* Upon occasion, a man had to manufacture his own hell-fire, either for himself or others: as one kind of home brew for the spirit's extremer voyages.

When Skelton's grandfather most kindly bailed him out and Skelton had returned Jakey Roberts's copy of *Swank* to him and turned down his grandfather's doubtlessly well-meant suggestion that they talk, and gone home to his fuselage, his private stock of hell-fire began to rise as volatile as rubbing spirits from the surfaces of his life.

Thou fool.

The odds and ends that lay around the interior of the fuselage, formerly in a skein of intimate connections that did not exclude himself, all began to separate amid cool segments of space. He felt the precise bevel at which his teeth rested against each other; and his hands lay in his lap within an invisible display case.

Hold on now, he told himself, no barking. For two hours he managed the control he needed, sitting as quietly at his breakfast table as a gyroscope. And then slowly the tramp of drilling winos came through his leafy window; and he wept with gratitude. When he had finished that, the salt and pepper shakers rejoined themselves to the table; the skein of connections returned and his hands sweated in one another's grasp.

He stepped outside, out to his garden fence, into the heart of the uproar. Standing by the hedge of uncleared vegetation, oleander cresting up out of it around one scrawny but wildly productive lime tree, he was point-blank to the marchers lurching mustily from left to right, while the drill sergeant marched backward ahead of them, surveying their primitive efforts with apoplectic eyes. Directly in front of Skelton, a younger, livelier wino passed; and each time the command changed, this wino found himself separated a few more feet from the others. Partly it was that he threw a good deal of florid body English into his marching; after each command, he would hunch his shoulders suddenly and stylishly like Fred Astaire, and slope further out of line. Finally, the drill sergeant stopped everything and realigned the preoccupied marcher, addressing him as "Fuckah!" in a lyrical tenor.

This kind of punctuating sight welded Skelton to reality as succinctly as an accident; but it drifted gauzily from his mind and he was isolated once more behind the hedge, irritably blinded by the glare of light off the fuselage. As usual, he looked at the lines in his palms.

Now this too: if his grandfather had not been in

such a goddamn hurry, he could have got a bondsman to make his bail and been done with the thing until his trial. Instead, there would have to be a conference with the old dizzard in which the shit was perfectly certain to hit the fan.

Finally, the younger wino was expelled from the march. He was out of breath.

"You're the one lives in the bomb," he said, pointing to the fuselage. Skelton nodded.

"Yes, that's me."

The young man said, raising his fingers to a seemingly deliquescent cheek: "My grandfather was decorated in the First World War."

"Oh yes . . ."

"Ask me why he was decorated."

"Why was he decorated?"

"I don't know."

Skelton thought: I want to live on the bottom of the sea. Nincompoops assault me in squads. The younger wino went off, taking the sergeant aside, and was pointing at Skelton; probably telling him: Commie, or meter smasher.

The sergeant came over. He had a peaceful, phlegmatic face, the face of a herbivore. "What's your game?" he asked.

"I'm a moonshiner."

"Well, more power to you. We're running a works of our own up in the joint there. I made the coil myself. Last batch I run off kicked the hydrometer out on the floor. It was like rocket fuel."

"I'd like to try it."

"I'd offer you a drop; but these useless mothers over here have went through it quick as snot on a bottle. A man went blind here before I took over the still. But I run a tight, clean ship."

Skelton looked over at the useless mothers. They were milling among fallen palm leaves, quite as lost as babies in the shadow of a half-boarded-up house with a moonshine works in its attic.

Well, thought Skelton, life looked straight in the eye was insupportable, as everyone knew by instinct. The great trick, contrary to the consensus of philosophy, is to avoid looking it straight in the eye. Everything askance and it all shines on.

But in general he felt recovered; or in any event, at rest in a reasonably cool aftermath. He went inside to take out the trash, adding everything conceivably trash to the contents of the galvanized barrel, including a painting Spacey Tracy, the Day-Glo Dago, had given him on Simonton Street, depicting a tall thermos bottle standing in a field of breath mints. This same artist had done a series of "contemporary" portraits of historical figures. Kafka as remittance man. Van Gogh clipping coupons by the sea. Dostoevsky with a four-foot string of credit cards. San Juan de la Cruz peering out of a condominium as though room service had used cheap Triple Sec in his margarita. Into the shitcan with everything ironic for the fun of it.

CARTER AND DANCE ARE IN THE BAIT SHACK and have told Myron Moorhen, the lickspittle accountant, to haul ass and give them the desk. They take one of his yellow legal sheets out and try to figure some way of salvaging Dance's winter guiding schedule even though he is no longer the owner of a guide boat. First they determine how long it will take to have a new skiff built up, how long the insurance will take to settle on the old one; as against the number of days that Carter is not booked and Dance is—so that Dance can use his skiff.

"There will have to be a small usage charge," says Carter.

"Naturally, man."

"Lemme tote this here up now." He ran his fingernail up and down the columns of numbers.

"What do you come up with?"

"You look."

"Hm."

"Don't look good."

"Sure don't. It looks sorta rank."

"How're you fixed now, Nichol."

Dance looked at him. "How'm I fixed?"

"That's what I ast."

"Cart, if turkeys was goin for one cent a pound I couldn't buy a raffle ticket on a jaybird's ass."

"*Haw haw hawmmm.*"

"If ten cent'd buy a tuxedo for a elerfunt, I couldn't buy a T-shirt for a flea."

"*Heeheehee.* Okay now. Let's, seriously now . . ."

Anyone else could have seen that Carter didn't care about these jokes; and in his strenuous laughter for the benefit of a man who had learned or stolen everything he knew and now wanted the use of his skiff, there was the very faintest yet palpable hint of the craven.

"Are you going to get around to doing something about that boy?" Carter asked; he liked Skelton well enough, but now by Christ things were getting to be an inconvenience.

"It's in the hands of the law," said Dance. "I mean not that I didn't give some thought to shooting him. But since I failed to shoot myself that day, I've kinda had a loss of innerest in shooting anything else."

"*Heeheeheemmmm.*"

"I might could take a notion though. If this brand of

irritation runs on I mean. He wasn't a bad kind of a kid."

"He wanted to guide."

"I know, I know."

Suddenly Carter saw how to ingratiate himself. "*We was just sendin him to the school of hard knocks, Nichol!*"

Now it was Dance's turn to laugh. The little joke was such a success that it pushed Carter clear through to the other side of his mild instinct for ingratiation. He thought again of Skelton and the schooling they had given him; and did not feel particularly good about it. Nevertheless, as a major-league brown-nose, he was unprepared to investigate the emotion.

THE PHONE RANG AND HE RAN BACK INTO THE fuselage. It was his mother. "Your grandfather would like you to come over here after dinner tonight."

"I'd just love to!"

"All right now."

"I'll be there, Ma, with bells on."

"But be here."

"THE FRENCH HAVE A WORD FOR IT," REmarked his grandfather, his back toward the woman as he mixed a drink; presently he turned and proffered the grog. "I call it pussy." His hands closed before him in a prayerful shape.

"I know you do, Goldsboro."

They were in old man Skelton's exercise room, whose variety of health machines seemed compromised by the presence of a well-stocked bar.

"I call it that because it is candid to call it that and I

am a candid man because I have nothing to hide."

"You won't get a whole lot of agreement about that in Key West, Goldsboro," said the lady. She was fifty and heavy. Her name was Bella Knowles. Her husband, an insurance broker who dabbled in gunrunning, now made his home on the Isle of Pines.

He said, "I was trying out that tone before I talk to my grandson. I have got to set that little smartbutt on the straight and narrow or he will end up in a bassinet like his old man."

"You should have let him go to jail rather than hang out with charter-boat fishermen."

"Hurry up with your drink. I'm fixing to carry on." He sat on the edge of the trampoline that dominated the room. Light from high, milky windows flooded into the little gym.

"I'll sip as long as I please."

"Long as you sip fast!"

"You're talking to a lady and the only one you'll ever get." Goldsboro Skelton rolled the medicine ball off the tremulous surface of the trampoline; it slumped to the floor.

"Well..."

The strange couple—the etiolated, successful crook and the rounded helpmeet of an imprisoned gunrunner —undressed without ceremony, the rickety and the ample in curious counterpart as they bent to slide off socks.

Playfully, Goldsboro Skelton, Cuban bullet holes still dimpling his hind end, mounted the trampoline and began to hop around, veinous fists clenched next to his ears in simple heroics. Now he was making some fairly impressive leaps, not ignored by Bella Knowles. She joined him.

At first they bounced in an irregular pattern, Skelton going up at the moment Bella touched down. They stopped for a moment toe to toe and fiddled with one another, and then began to bound again, this time in the same rhythm. As they each looked at the leaping and speeding against the far wall, Goldsboro Skelton was an arrow of capability to Bella Knowles, a pinksurge of desire.

Beneath them, the black iron perimeter of the trampoline enlarged and contracted with their bounds. The thousands of springs that held its canvas surface squeaked like lemmings, unlubed harquebus locks or tholepins.

Then they collided, recoiled apart, bounced each unequally through high air to a delirium of limbs, glanced off the trampoline, and crashed to the floor.

They lay without motion. Reassured gym flies began to whirl in the light of the high windows once more. At that moment, Goldsboro Skelton's grandson was reading the part in Pliny's *Natural History* where the swell of tide at moon's rising among the stars is described. And in other respects, life went on, though it seemed largely unassured here in the gym.

Presently Goldsboro Skelton began to crawl immediately behind his own nosebleed toward Bella Knowles. When he got to her he looked at her open eyes above the terribly fattened lip. Skelton staggered to his feet for a glass of water, which he held tenderly to her mouth. "The French have a word for this," he remarked with some preoccupation.

"What is it, you cheesy piece of bung fodder?" Bella Knowles inquired.

AT DUSK, THE LIGHT CAN'T GET MUCH PAST Carlos's market on Elizabeth Street; so when you walk down Eaton to go to Skelton's mother's house, and look down William Street or Elizabeth Street, the shrimp boats are crowded hugely in the shadow of those streets while the clouds of gulls above them soar in sunlight; and on the corners, palm leaves that are piled for pickup and that rattle all day with lizards in the warmth now are cool and quiet.

When you pass the corner of Simonton, the mail trucks are backed up to bays that are closed with corrugated doors, and at least one boy is doing a figure eight in the quiet parking lot on his bicycle; and the glass and iron pineapples on the gate at the Carriage Trade look like scarabs held in old silver.

Duval Street, crowded and Latin all day, now seems filled with space and breeze, serenely modified by a taxicab spinning along in golden light; and the ticket seller at the dirty-movie house graciously promises the drill sergeant "no less than twenty fuck scenes." From a boat, Key West would seem to have shrunk once more unto the sea. And the few boats that have gone out to night drift for tarpon in the channels carry their red and green running lights through the blackness sweetly.

Dinner would still be transpiring at his parents' house, borne upon crazy accusations by his grandfather and Dada rebuttals by his father; his mother taking a view not less than Olympian of this particular, by now ancient, squabble.

So Skelton slipped into their garage and got his fishing rod, walked half a block to the corner of Front Street to the Dos Amigos bar, had a single bourbon and water, shot one maladroit game of eight-ball with a counterrevolutionary Cuban shrimper who claimed to be able to navigate from here to the north coast of Haiti without chart or sounding because "I am a Key West captain"; then took up his rod and crossed Front Street at last light and walked down to the pocket beach that lay between the fabric factory and Tony's restaurant.

It was dark and warm as summer, and tarpon were assailing bait under the restaurant lights; there were maybe a couple of dozen fish striking the lit-up water and shrimp were clearing the water completely and kicking out into the darkness.

Directly above the fish, on the corner of a balustrade, a man in a white dinner jacket was pressing at a girl in a gown, hauling her against the iron balcony, mashing into her with his face and holding his cocktail perfectly balanced out over the ocean without looking at it.

"Natalie."

"Gordon."

Skelton climbed out onto the transom of a half-beached skiff and chopped a cast right into the working bait from his lair in the darkness. He made one strip and came up tight on a tarpon. The heavy fish just held its own a moment, trying to think what had happened; then it vaulted high and terrific into the light, right up clear to where its gills rattled alongside the balustrade.

Gordon spun; and Natalie dropped her jaw. Gordon glanced ornery into his empty glass, looked at Skelton's line trailing into the darkness, and led "Nat" to an empty table inside, his moment quite gone.

Skelton cupped the reel handles, broke the fish off, reeled up; and headed back to the house feeling an exquisite synthesis of spirit and place. His grandfather would possibly be there with his secretary, Bella Knowles, rotating her wry, discerning face and the spit curls that had adorned her temples for nearly forty years. Skelton wondered how many gallons of saliva that must have required.

He walked in through the gate without knocking.

At the end of the porch, he could see his grandfather without his secretary eating in the lighted breakfast room. His father was on the porch, beneath his netting; with the television shoved under one end. He pulled up an iron chair and sat next to his father, who in a moment glanced at Skelton and said, "Green Bay missed the extra point." A few minutes later, he leaned forward and turned down the sound. "Green Bay has got great flankers," he told his son. "But Jesus, Macarthur Lane is some running-back. He's got these lateral moves right at the line of scrimmage that don't seem physically possible. —Watch now: this close to the end zone, the linebackers will be keying off the running-backs." Touchdown. The linebackers keyed off the running-backs; but the quarterback threw the ball.

"I'll be a sonofabitch," said his father. He looked at his son. "Do me a favor."

"Name it."

"Get off the violence. You're too romantic to be any good at it. This bird Dance will eat you alive. He knows how to do violence and you're a dilettante at it."

Skelton thought with some admiration that Dance's trick had been a well-organized bit of cruelty. The touch of authenticity had been the story of Charlie Starkweather, who Skelton remembered as a kind of anachronistic dry-gulch artist running through the West; who got wired to a Nebraska utility outlet in a metal chair by officials of the republic. Restaurants darkened and Starkweather went off like a flashbulb at Tricia's wedding. It reduced his bulk through vaporization. He no longer fitted the electrical collar. They found him in the goodbye room like a wind-torn 1890 umbrella. A year later he might have grown Virginia creeper like a grape stake. After each electrocution, the officials of the republic get together for a real down-home Christian burial out of that indomitable American conviction that even God likes fried food.

"I didn't know you had this affection for violence," said his father as humor, studying his eyes gone vague beneath his Starkweather revery.

"I don't."

"Had you been emotionally forced into it?"

"More or less."

"Are you going to admit it?"

"No. I'm not going to pay for it either."

"I can't imagine this happening among scientists."

"I'm not a scientist and I'm not going to be one. It takes all the brains I've got to figure out where game fish keep themselves."

"And you never got into these cross fires until you started reading French poets. Furthermore, when your grandfather offered to bail you out, you didn't make yourself plausible to him by asking him to bring your Apollinaire instead."

"Well, he didn't know what I was talking about. Jakey Roberts gave me his copy of *Swank* and I read a short history of Spanish fly instead of *L'Hérésiarque et Cie.*"

"Those frog lunatics have produced a generation of destructive addlepates to which I fear you appending yourself. Though I'd prefer it to your fiddling with dope, it's a narrow choice."

Little does he know, thought Skelton.

The two men laughed; possibly close to tears. Skelton peeled up one end of the netting and twisted it over the corner of the frame. "That's not true." He could look at his father.

"What's not?" his father asked.

"About Apollinaire and the others."

"Don't you think?"

"I'd say Nietzsche produced more addlepates."

"What about Gurdjieff and Ouspensky?"

"What about Kahlil Gibran?"

"What about Tex Ritter?" And so on through Father Coughlin, Darius Milhaud, Stockhausen, Donald Duck, Baba Ram Dass, Lenin, a certain Bürgermeister in a Milwaukee beer ad, guitar fops from the hideous 1960s, Thomas Edison—and more laughter. Then, mock serious, his father took up his violin and played the opening of *Corrinne Corrina* hillbilly style and beautiful. Skelton lit a powdery Dutch cigar and listened in a swoon of those sad clodhopper strains, dying day, newspaper boys yelling faintly as they filled their baskets; a swoon that was as much as anything a part of his more than trifling instinct for some kind of topographical perspective upon his own life, as against a vision of cycling chemicals in a closed system that somehow never explained the attrition of the things that ail you.

He could hear the quarterback now calling signals in the new style: "Blue! Right! Get back! Eighty! Red!" *Snap.* The play was underway. The quarterback rolled out in a fake draw.

SKELTON'S GRANDFATHER STEPPED ONTO THE porch in a fog of cooking smells and looked across at the two of them talking with an air of reconnaissance. He made a minute adjustment of his shoulders before coming over.

"What happened to your nose, Gramp?" Skelton asked. His grandfather raised fingers to the swollen bridge.

"Damn trunk lid on my Coupe de Ville popped up and got my beezer."

A hand reached out of the bed, tugged the mosquito netting free, and drew it down over the opening. A moment later, they heard the television; Green Bay had the ball on their own forty-nine.

"Guess who I just had a drink with," said the grandfather to Skelton.

"Can't."

"Nichol Dance."

"Ah, then."

"Now I had had a look into that boy's insurance situation and learned he wasn't going to be out a dime. So, I told him if he wanted you in court I would see him in hell first but I would at least run him clean out of Monroe County on a rail. I asked him, I said, 'Mr. Dance, are you a gambler?' And he said no he was not and so I told him, 'Mr. Dance, let the insurance company handle your woes.' I had backed myself up with a transcript of his criminal record. I suppose you know he is vicious."

"I guess I did."

"Anyway, he is a lively boy with a mean streak in him. But he listens to reason. He's part of the community and so he'll have to do like I told him."

"Do you want a chair?"

"No. —Now what were you doing with his boat?"

"Guiding."

"You haven't dropped that yet?"

"Not going to."

"How much would it cost to have your own boat?"

"About four grand if you have it built and powered right."

"You want me to stake you?"

"Sure. Ha. Ha."

"How would you pay me back? And don't laugh so fast."

"Out of my guiding fees."

"I'd doubt that except Dance told me you'd make a great skiff guide. I guess you're on."

When Skelton's grandfather meant every word he was saying, he talked to you belly to belly, eyes looking through yours; if he had a drink, he crimped it high and close and emphasized his sentences by the gentle knuckle bumps against your sternum. He was a winning man, so far from schizophrenia that a thousand pitiful losers knew no more than to give him their money. Skelton's father, listening, said, "Generation after generation, the blind leading the blind. It gives them something to do."

IN HIS BACK YARD AND UNDER A TORTUOUS, UNleafed poinciana, Nichol Dance was removing slabs of amberjack from a tray of brine and laying them across rough wire racks inside a gutted refrigerator that he used as a smoker. He was feeling stupid, real dumb in fact.

He had a good little fire of buttonwood coals going and the rich dark amberjack would smoke down to just the right moisture. But he was making work for himself, filleting and brining all that fish meat; and, in general, not feeling very bright, maybe even, you know, *dumb*.

What I need, he thought, is some credence; because damned if I'm not getting pushed out of shape around here. Skiff all burnt to shit and that old crud telling me to wait on the insurance. *Damn.*

And now work to do. Bad but necessary work to do based on his and Carter's dismal, yes he saw that now, dismal and stupid joke that he as well as anybody knew was so steeped in locker-room fatuity that when it backfired and his boat went up in flames, he and Cart, unable to escape the joke, had instead to hunt all over that canal, pistol in hand tumid with their own shared rage, vacant as any emotion based in property.

But Dance was convinced that there was a necessity independent of what was right. Sometimes you did a wrong thing but then it was done and there you were. Damned if you weren't—so best thing was, just rest your ass. The time to take your lumps would soon enough be at hand. Dance wished he hadn't set Skelton up like he had; but it was done and now he had to follow through. He thought he was a nice enough boy. Nichol Dance *truly* hoped he wouldn't have to waste him.

So the pistol was slipped into the front of his pants, butt to the right, and a short-sleeved shirt (blue porpoises on a white background) outside his trousers concealed it all. Naturally, the pistol was uncomfortable; but it was credence and collateral in the most liquid form he knew. It answered the problem of what came in handy when you had to follow through.

He stopped on the way out and looked at himself in the oval hall window. What's happening to this boy? he wondered.

Sometimes, he thought, you just wander around not feeling very smart and your clothes aren't sharp and your car is a loser and you know you haven't done a thing you will be remembered for and you haven't got no more sense than a curbstone nor brains enough to come in out of the rain or quit playing the dumb gags that only lead from one atrocity to the next. And you *just feel dumb*.

In the drive, he stopped and felt the south wind lifting the trees, warm as Cuba, and knew the fish were rolling in the channels, young moon and easy tides. I'm a boy without a future, he thought with a smile. I bought a Ford when I should've bought a Chevrolet.

SKELTON AND MIRANDA MET AT MALLORY PIER
for sunset. A red sun was palpably completing its arc to
the left of Man and Woman keys; in another couple of
months, it would drop off by Mule and Archer keys. It
would be hours after dinner and scratch-baseball games
would be audible all through the city. Now a crowd of
freaks waited for this thing to happen.

"Are you still upset?"

"About your old boyfriend? No. Not too much.
Will I always have to be used to that?"

"Not if it's important."

There was an old converted liberty ship, now of
Grand Cayman registry. A cucumber boat, someone
said. It was moored at the fuel dock. Three muscular
men in T-shirts hung over the fantail looking at the sunset hippie girls loose-titted in their ersatz Oshkosh By
Gosh work rags. The conch-salad man glided by yelling "When you're hot you're hot! When you're not,
you're not!" to strengthen his claims for the aphrodisi-
acal qualities of the conch salad he sold from the front
basket of his bike.

"If he's right about that conch salad," Skelton said,
"it's the last thing these crazy fuckers need."

The hot red sun began to penetrate the pale curve of
sea, flaring optically at the thin line of division; the line
gradually rose until only the smallest flame rested on the
horizon; and snuffed. Applause rose.

"Come to my place tonight," said Skelton.

"If you'd like."

They walked up Caroline and cut across Margaret
to Skelton's block. There was a south wind and Skelton
was saying that with these new-moon tides there ought
to be some fish moving. Miranda told him that she

thought—she said it pleasantly—that he ought to be able to enjoy a south wind, the new moon, and swimming fish without having to go out and catch something.

"Pretty esoteric."

"What kind of music are you going to woo me with?"

"Pachanga from Radio Free Habana."

Miranda had a springy step. Let us compare her mouth, thought Skelton, to a delicate section of tangerine. Who said that kissing was sucking on a thirty-foot tube the last five feet of which were full of shit? It was not to the point who said it. Right frame of mind, he thought, surreptitiously looking at the lovely young girl, I'd bite on either end.

Pausing sternly across from Key West Oxygen and Ambulance, Skelton swept Miranda into his arms and sucked at the tangerine-like end of the thirty-foot tube, never heeding what might have been at its other end, doubtless rising slowly toward his mouth.

They turned into Skelton's lane; where a car was parked at the lane's junction with Margaret Street. Skelton walked another twenty feet before he stopped and looked back at the car. Its frenched headlights, bubble skirts, dummy baby spotlights, tinted glass, bull-nosed hood, and rust declared it to be Nichol Dance's.

"Miranda, you're gonna have to go."

"How come? I just walked ten blocks."

"I can't take the chance," said Skelton half to himself.

"Shall I have my tubes tied?"

"That isn't what I mean," he said, staring past and around the car. "The truth is, Miranda, there's a man around here belongs to that car who doesn't like me."

"You're worried."

"I really am." Maybe he was.

"Wouldn't you like me to wait."

"I don't think so."

"Okay . . . be careful."

"It's not that serious, Miranda. It certainly may not be, in any case."

"Okay . . ."

"I hate to miss out, I mean . . ."

"You'll get another shot," she said, adding though, "Possibly not." She started down the lane for Margaret Street. Now Skelton just put his hands in his pockets and thought, Where is that sly mother hiding himself.

The shadows lay this way and that, the way a tide will carry on a particularly shaped bottom, bulging and deepening and only holding fish in specific places. Or the way six grandmothers will fall when simultaneously struck by lightning.

So Skelton watched that way, at the ledges of shadow behind the wino hotel, behind the pile of dry-rotted cypress planking and iron salvage; and for long moments, he just looked for motion. And tried not to think of trifles.

Violence. Why did this stillness go so well with violence? Like cupping your ear in the high wind to make a pocket of quiet. The palm leaves moved and sent bony fingers of shadow across the ground; and detailed shadows gave way to vacancy. And notionally, you see your spirit escape like smoke from a familiar corpse.

He slipped over alongside the car and looked inside. Nothing. A bonefish net lay across the back seat. A curved plane of reflected moonlight divided the dashboard into bright and dark isosceles triangles.

Where is that hillbilly sonofabitch, or whatever he is. That Hoosier dipshit.

Skelton decided to just go in the house and wait and

see. Lock the door, locate a well-made paring knife that was destined to see other than cucumber in this karma. Lift an eye to the sill and get the drop on that crime monger.

I suppose you know he's vicious.

No one was in the yard either. He looked next door. There were three lighted windows in the hotel, each with a silhouetted wino like a playing card. I bid three winos.

The boat burns once more in his mind. All that Nichol Dance owned, with the gas tank blowing sideways through the hull. Quicksink, scream of superheated gas, destruction bubbles, loss.

The boat sails against the moon, a gunman in the bow, sails and circles into the light, into the dark, into the light. The creak of his own breath.

Skelton opened the door of the fuselage and went in.

Nichol Dance said, "Turn on the light and sit down."

"How're you doing?" Skelton asked. Dance was doing his level best to look like the Antichrist.

"Not bad, not bad. Lost my boat. But apart from that, not too awful."

"What's the gun for?"

"I just wanted you to see what I would blow your head off with if you ever tried to guide out of any dock west of Marathon. Now you gawn and fill in the blanks."

"Big Pine, Little Torch, Sugarloaf, Key West."

"Amo ignore your little shit-ass joke and about halfway assume you got this deal crystal-clear," Dance said, frittering with the Colt's hammer.

"Right you are."

Dance was thinking, He understands me but it don't seem I got all that much credence.

"I have notched thisere pistol oncet," he said mea-
gerly.

"Yes, yes I heard."

Dance was momentarily unable to speak. He felt
that in using the killing of the exercise boy to establish
credence here he had made a lie of all his penitence.

"So, I guess I'll be on my way."

"Okay, so long."

Skelton got up and excused himself, squeezed past
Nichol Dance and out the door, and ran down the lane
toward Margaret Street. "Miranda! Wait up!"

Dance, bemused, sat and wondered when the last
time was he could say he'd had some honest-to-god credence, and not the kind of cheapjack reasonable fac-
simile thereof he'd just brought out for display.

INTELLIGENT MORNING: INDIAN RIVER ORANGE
juice, thousand-times-washed Levi's, perfect Cuban
guayabera shirt, Eric Clapton on the radio, sunlight
swimming the walls, cucarachas running a four-forty
in the breadbox, mockingbirds doing an infinitely delicate imitation of mockingbirds. Yes, gentlemen, there is
next to nothing; but I'm going to have fun anyway.

Now simply for the hell of it, let's see what Jesus is
up to today. Skelton the Bible jock pulled down his
Good Book and read for a half hour to see what would
catch the mind. A sunshine morning for ordering a skiff,
radio daydreams, and Bible reading. Better wake Miranda. Matthew 9:13. *I will have mercy, and not sacri-
fice: for I am not come to call the righteous.*

"Miranda honey!"

"Turn down the radio, Tom, just a little."

"If you say."

"Just a little. Thanks. Who is that?"

"Derek and the Dominos."

"What time is it?"

"Seven-thirty. Want some Cheerios?"

"Sure, let me dress now, I've just got time. Seventh-grade geography in an hour."

Skelton the spy: the gloom of women dressing. The swell of buttocks where they glide into back, vanishing under swoop of Indian cotton blouse. Turn for sleepy smile. Demiglobes of breast in blouse, pale half of moon belly, gone under the advance of mother-of-pearl buttons. It is summer in Russia; I am preparing for a mortal duel in a swoon of girls. Miranda the pale.

Skelton bent to the raining Cheerios. Calm yourself. Love, knowledge, Jesus, ocean, cunt, and harmless victory. Try to think of more things at once. A richness of reference. Old friends of the family smothering in W-2 forms. I have wiped my butt with a sheet of personal numerals. What was Count Tolstoy's social security number? If you don't answer that in one second, the Republic is Dead.

Miranda came in from the fresh air.

"Who are those men out there?"

"Winos."

"Do they always march?"

"Just recently."

Sometimes from the hotel you could hear ping-pong players, radios, cats, fighting, seagulls, and the failure of simple machinery. The hotel was surrounded and in effect seized by vegetation in every form; and on winter days the wind would occasionally bend each leaf at a certain angle to the sun and the whole would seem to combust with vegetable light and glitter. The drunks responded to this magnificence and moved about the miserable lawn, eyes squinted, in an impressive rummy minuet.

Skelton remembered singing in kindergarten:

> "*The Blue Danube Waltz,*
> *By Strauss, By Strauss . . .*"

"Well, I have to go. Do I look all right?"

"You look great."

"Don't have my books. I'll wing it in geography."

"Tell them the Miami oölite doesn't run southwest of Big Pine."

"Can't. We're still on the East Coast alluvial shelf. Besides, what you say isn't quite true. You're thinking of Key Largo limestone."

"Sure felt good!" Skelton said at the door.

Said Miranda, "I'll see you at Mallory dock one of these days."

Nine o'clock. Thomas Skelton started for Powell's Boat Shop. He was feeling the first wonder of living in a town where there is someone who wouldn't mind killing you. That truly gave a community subjective structure. They laughed at my killer dildo when I drove deep into the lasagna. Pipkins of menace were scattered on the Navajo. Yes, thought Skelton, I am giddy with anticipation and not in the least slowed down by seven instances of having my ashes hauled in the previous eight hours.

POWELL WAS IDLING IN THE FRONT OF HIS SHOP, fitting a replacement iron to an eight-inch lignum-vitae jack plane. He looked up over his glasses.

"Is what I hear true?"

"About what?"

"Nichol's skiff?"

"Not hardly." Tom smiled.

"Hm."

Powell brushed the sawdust off his bench, then set the jack plane next to two sharply radiused rock-maple spar planes, their irons bright under a coat of 3-in-One oil.

"Are you building now, James?"

"Nosuh."

"Feel like it?"

"Do I feel like building what, Tom?"

"Guide skiff."

"Well, can you pay for it?"

"Yes, sir."

"I expect old Dance is going to be in here after one as soon as he hears from the inshawrance."

"Well, this is a firm order, James."

Powell put down the plane and picked up a broad carpenter's pencil and a pad of paper from Tropical Sheet Metal on Green Street. Skelton was dizzy with pleasure.

They laid the skiff out along the firm edges of Skelton's daydreams, not in any way sparing the horses. They would start with a rough glass hull sent down from the mainland, build it up, and finish it.

"It's the hull I want, James. It rides rough and has too steep an entry forward. But it poles good. It won't sail and still floats in dew."

"What does the hull look like when we get it?"

"Rough."

"Is it cut down to the shear line?"

"No. There's a scribe."

"I guess I'll go through a bunch of saber-saw blades. What about the transom?"

"Twenty-one inches."

"Well, I can electroplane that to where we need it. What about live wells?"

"They come attached. The ones I've seen were

through-bolted in five places and glassed directly to the transom."

"All right. Now let's lay the sonofabitch out. You want to do it in half-inch?"

"No, three-quarter."

"That stuff goes for an arm and a leg now!"

Skelton's happiness was hard to hide. When you thought there was nothing, this was one of the things there was. For example.

He sketched on the scratch pad for a few minutes.

"That's how I want it aft: three hatches with interconnected waterways routed in a taper so they drain to the sump—"

"All right."

"—and all hardware flush-mounted to a drive fit—"

"All right."

"—and maybe a half-inch overhang above that aft bulkhead."

"All right."

"Now in the corners of that same bulkhead, let's run the self-bailing drainage through PVC pipe, you know, right through the dry storage and into the sump like the waterways."

"All right."

"Now gunwales. Average width about seven inches, faired back from the forward casting deck to the livewell lids."

"You want it all flush, right? No drop to the casting deck?"

"None. The fuel is forward. The controls are forward. So the forward bulkhead is vented; and the overflow is starboard a few inches under the gunwale."

"All right. Let me tote up the materials and we'll make that your deposit. Have I got your telephone number?"

"It's in the book. —Now, anything there that throws you? —I'm just asking."

"I've laid a thousand miles of teak on a radius. This here is all right angles and butt blocks. There isn't a Dutchman in that kind of work when yours truly is the carpenter. So save your last question for some jackleg of your acquaintance."

SKELTON STEPPED UP ONTO THE PORCH AND looked under the net. His father was sound asleep, a volume of Huizinga on his chest; he seemed not so much to have dozed off as to be in a deep, granitic slumber from which he could not easily have awakened.

In the kitchen, his mother was reading Brillat-Savarin, learning about what his grandfather, the high-leaping Goldsboro Skelton, would call nigger food. It was surprising to find her home in the afternoon, or at least, home alone. She had so many friends whom she served as confessor and adviser. Her contact and its attendant gusts of energy created addiction among her coevals for whom she was the sole connection.

"Daddy looks exhausted."

"He is!"

Skelton looked at her. Her hair was turned up in a twist behind, a vigorous, plaited gray.

"Meaning what?"

"Your father has been out all-night-long."

"Come on."

"You walked into the house at the moment I thought to tell you. Another half hour and I would have changed my mind."

"Is this the first time?"

"No. It's been going on for months."

Skelton asked with fear: "What does he do?"

"I suspect it's a girlfriend. I suppose sex is the only thing that would make *me* get up after seven months of making an ass of myself."

She loved to get Skelton on the edge of his seat so that every word dropped like a stone on a sheet of tin. Counterploy:

"He could be performing Acts of Christian Mercy," he said.

"Maybe he's learning to be a fishing guide," she said, taking the trick.

"I'm not the one who isn't keeping him at home."

"What other unkindness pops into your mind?"

"You started it."

Glowering rises and fades.

Finally Skelton inquired, "What's his explanation?"

"He doesn't know I know. I haven't really . . . I mean I can't quite think what to say. For all I know, he's been out every night since he first got into that . . ."

"Bassinet."

NO MOTHER DOG TURNING AN EXPECTANT NOSE to a garbage pail filled from top to bottom with racks of spring lamb ever felt a surer sense of unoccluded fortune than Skelton contemplating his skiff, Miranda, and his father abroad in the night. As to this last, yes, it was a mixed blessing. Perhaps he was having at a tart in the lower purlieus of Duval; perhaps her name was Mona and she drowned a man at the Muff Diver's Ball instead of merely washing his face as her calling card promised. And yes, the infidelities of an aging lame from a Key West bassinet were a sorry prospect when the lame was your very own progenitor. But there is a life that is not a life, in which the more adamant obstructions of the heart masquerade as loss, dreams, or carburetor trouble. A silent man wastes his own swerve of molecules; just as a bee "doing its number on the flower" is as gone to history as if it never was. The thing and its expression are to be found shaking hands at precisely that point where Neverneverland and Illyria collide with the Book of Revelation under that downpour of grackle droppings that is the present at any given time.

Skelton was walking to his grandfather's office on Eaton Street on a morning so full of heat and light that traffic seemed composed of wet, swollen cars. A carpenter rebuilding a porch along Skelton's way dropped his wrecking bar and it rang like a bell. With each breath you got more for your money. He passed the library where thoughtful ladies held the fort and said good morning to a man carrying a cockatoo in a white enameled cage; no one could have avoided the resemblance of the ring-like brilliant eyes of the cockatoo to those of its owner. The bird made some snarky remark; and Skelton gave it a small compulsive wave, regretting it immediately.

Skelton had no way of knowing that the man's name was also Thomas Skelton (no kin), though he had seen the name in the telephone book and wondered if it mightn't be some distant connection of his family's (not).

When the sun first assembles itself over the broken skyline of Key West on a morning of great humidity, a thunderous light fills the city and everyone moves in stately flotation through streets that are conduits of something empyrean. Also, things can get sweaty.

JAMES POWELL, THE BOATBUILDER, HAD CALLED with the cost of materials and Skelton was going to take his grandfather up on his kind offer of cash money.

The "Skelton Building" on Eaton Street was a two-story frame house whose formerly domestic rooms were now the world's most gerrymandered office, with the stenographer, for example, working out of an upstairs bedroom filled with war-surplus filing cabinets; and an accountant with the only abacus in Key West busy in the old music room under a ceiling full of putti and cherubs in the school of Rubens out of *The Saturday Evening Post*. At one time, Goldsboro Skelton had felt the need of safes; and so whole rooms were filled with them, combinations lost and hinges rusted to inutility. In the front-hall closet, a ragged hole showed where a small Diebold Chicago Universal safe with a rainbow on its door had shot through the floor and into the cistern, probably killing frogs.

In the front hall, directly behind the front door, Bella Knowles abused visitors from a low mahogany desk whose bland surface held five Princess Phones like a relief model of the Caribbean. Every time the door opened, she was revealed in amazing proximity to people passing on the sidewalk, really only a few feet away, her eyes at rump level.

Goldsboro Skelton himself ran his curious and impalpable island empire from an old water closet, a generous one of the Victorian years, whose pipes and dainty crapper had been replaced with horizontal writing surfaces for the signing of checks and those letters of business which in a republic more perfect than the one here in Hotcakesland would be actionable matters of extortion.

"Hello, Thomas," said Bella Knowles. "I suppose you're here for money."

"Do you."

"Aren't you?"

"What?"

"Here for money?"

"Are you talking to me?"

"Yes!"

"Oh . . . here for money? No no no. To see my grandfather, Missus uh . . ."

"Knowles."

"Right. And uh anything transpiring between my grandfather and I is just liable to be none of your business!"

"Now, now."

"Is he alone?"

"Yes he is."

"I'll just go in then."

"I'll buzz him."

"Don't bother."

"I'LL JUST BUZZ HIM."

"Well, whatever gets you off, Missus . . ."

"Knowles."

"Hey! I read that the hubby's being released from Cuba—"

"Yes he is."

"Gee, I suppose it's been awful with the uh cat away so long."

"Awful."

In the imperceptible moment of actual crossing of the grandfather's threshold, Skelton realized he was off on the wrong foot; and he quickly balanced the irritation with the fact that James Powell had ordered the materials.

"Sit down, Tom. I'll be with you in a moment."

Skelton waited standing until his grandfather looked up from his papers with a wordless interrogative glance.

"Well, the boat is underway," Skelton said with, for some reason, embarrassment. There was a pause.

"I'm sorry, I don't follow."

"James Powell is starting my guide skiff."

"Right . . . ?"

"Well, you said you would lend me the money."

"When?" he said, quick. "When did I say that?"

"The other night," said Skelton nearly inaudible.

"Oh God, let me look through my books here a sec."

"If you don't want to lend me the money, say so."

Goldsboro Skelton leaped up in a rage: "I just bailed you out of the damn jail! How much do you want from an old man!"

Skelton walked out, passing Bella Knowles hurrying into the office. When Skelton was safely gone, she asked, "Was it about money?"

Well, face it, Skelton thought, you're screwed. How dear it would have been to me, he thought, to bust the old fart in the teeth; then rip the electrical cord out of the lamp and shove it one furlong up Bella Knowles's fundament and waggle the light switch until she blew her dentures out the skylight. Stuff like that. You know, mean.

Powell was in his shop fitting up a handsome little dunnage box out of teak mill ends, countersinking the screws and pegging them with plugs of mahogany dowel. Skelton was in an agony of embarrassment.

"James—"

"We're gonna have the hull in the morning!"

"I'm afraid not."

"Why? What?"

"The whole thing is off, James, I'm sorry."

Powell put down his tools a little angrily.

"What's a matter?"

"I don't have the money."

"*What!*" Powell laughed at him.

"I'm sorry, I don't."

"Your grandfather paid the whole thing this morning, material and labor in advance."

Skelton headed for the office again, resigned to a day of embarrassment.

MYRON MOORHEN THE ACCOUNTANT WAS AT the front window of the bait shack, his fingertips indenting slightly against the glass, looking out at the rain. The rain was coming down so heavily that it no longer seemed to move. Traffic hissed. It was a hot winter day.

Carter was leaning back in a chair next to a freezer, walking a penny between his fingers. Nichol Dance stood in the open doorway, the heavy rain falling just past the end of his nose like a curtain.

Carter said, "You've gone soft."

Dance, dejected, said, "Maybe so."

"Now you're out of it. Now what are you gonna do?"

Dance turned slowly, bored. "Caddy. I'm gonna be Jack Nicklaus's caddy. I'll have a V-neck sweater and at night I'll jack off in a hankie. My life will be simple but it will be complete."

"Come on, Nichol."

"What do you care?"

"I care because I give you ten days before it's fun with bottles and you out at Snipe Point trying to get around to shooting yourself."

"I suppose."

"I mean this is insulting."

"I suppose."

"I mean, didn't you forbid him to guide?"

"Yeah I did."

"Then how come James Powell is building him a

guide boat? I mean, now *you* can't get one built and **he's** gone to guide."

"I didn't forbid him to have a skiff built."

"What do you think he means to do with it!"

"I don't know, pull crab pots. I have to let him hang himself, if that's what he is gonna do. This is a democracy."

"God I don't know about you. Jese, I mean what are you planning when he guides, and it does look to me like he will when that boat is ready?"

"Didn't I told you?" Dance asked him impatiently. "I will shoot him!"

"That's what you *say!*"

"Hey, Cart?"

"What?"

"Why don't *you* do it, you got yourself so worked up?"

"Nichol! *I like him!*" Carter bustled around the freezer, then pointlessly opened it, drawing out a block of ice that imprisoned myriad silver fish. He held it to the light and looked. "Shoot!"

"Well, sergeant, how are you doing with those new men?"

"Not bad at all." The just-blown whistle hung from his neck, a concise scapular to the general chop-chop of getting from Point A to Point B in Hotcakesland.

The thunder of winos on the resonant staircases of the wooden hotel, their appearance, and the slow inexorable milling impressed themselves more upon Skelton than the subsequent extrusion of the insulted and injured through the cuneiforms of drill so indispensable to that choral oink we call the military. A small sea of the harmed poured onto the impromptu drill field; and as the sergeant's barks and whistles rang out, they began to move as a man.

TWO MEN, NOT ENTIRELY DISSIMILAR, WERE beginning the day under the bright scudding clouds of the southeast trades. Thomas Skelton, with his lust for affinities, was going to visit Miranda Cole. Nichol Dance, who so rued his life and the things that had come of it that he drove his entire rather complicated self through the needle's eye of a career in guiding—Nichol Dance was heading to Islamorada to buy a skiff.

The future cast a bright and luminous shadow over Thomas Skelton's fragmented past; for Dance, it was the past that cast the shadow. Both men were equally prey to mirages. Thomas Skelton required a sense of mortality; and, ironically, it was Nichol Dance who was giving it to him; for Skelton understood perfectly well that there was a chance, however small, that Nichol Dance would kill him. This faint shadow lay upon his life now as discreetly as the shadow of cancer lies among cells. And Skelton asked himself, not particularly thinking of an act of Dance's, shall I find it hard to die?

A sane man thinking of death, however casually, should immediately visit a girl whether in quest of information, affinities, or carnal gratification. It's a case of any port in a storm, mortality being, in any case, an omnipresent hurricane.

Miranda had the second floor of a boatbuilder's recollection of Greek architecture from a nineteenth-century schoolboy's primer, executed in Dade County pine and painted a virginal white.

Miranda was a Saturday-morning pastry cook, and met him at the door in an apron dusted with flour. Skelton followed her toward the kitchen, gazing at the rooms as he went. They were tall, rectilinear rooms with great transomed windows, cool with their own spacious and circulatory atmospheres. (The astronauts are nose to bung in their "capsules"; while Captain Nemo sat at an ormolu control console; and if the astronauts have a capsule, Nemo had a Duomo.)

The last room shy of the kitchen seemed the most inhabited, with its small walnut dining-room table and re-covered divan; under the table were the small pyramids of termite sawdust that in Key West must be swept up almost daily.

"I'm making a cake for the Pillsbury Bake-off." A handsome old kitchen; big windows looking into subtropical alleyways; a four-blade wooden fan with a bead chain, turning rather slowly now but displacing a wondrous amount of air full of baking smell. The stove was a restaurant-size Magic Chef, thirty or forty years old, black stars for burner grates and a control panel like one from an Hispano-Suiza, two ovens, and the whole covered in deep opalescent enamel with precise blue trim.

"What kind of cake?"

"It's sort of my invention."

"What's it like?"

"Hm, well, it resembles a gâteau de Savoie moka, except I'm using my version of a Viennese icing. I forget, do you cook?"

"Some Cuban dishes."

"I think we can have a look at this now."

Skelton was next to her as she drew open the oven door. The beautiful cake was on the wire rack, rising uniformly; but something was wrong. Miranda cried out. A mouse had got into the oven and sunk to its flanks in the cake; as the air hit it, the mouse burst into flames. Miranda seized a pair of pot holders and snatched the cake from the oven and put it atop the stove. The burning mouse smoked, then smoldered, and finally became a blackened emblem in the top of the cake. Gâteau rodentine.

Miranda said: "Jesus H. Christ."

"I'm sorry."

"Goddamn son of a bitch."

"I know, I know. What a shame."

Miranda slashed off the top of the cake; cut two big wedges out of the remainder and put them on plates with glasses of milk. They sat down and ate the cake. It was a kind of coffee sponge cake with an echo of lemon and butter; clear, and ethereal.

Miranda's hands were resting on the table, one a fist, the other open flat on the walnut, shapely with short clear fingernails, a part where you could read out the whole physical presence.

Afternoon subsides in a golden burst of sunlight and the smell of coffee. Skelton observes a tripartite composition in rich pre-Raphaelite pastels: a band of blue sky, and a band of baby clouds traversing slowly toward the right, the deeply radiused orbs of Miranda's bottom. Skelton lifts his cheek from the firm musculature at the small of her back and reverently brushes with his lips the flattened node of coccyx; a gesture at the point of a hip and she turns over, gray eyes grazing away to a white flash of gull in the upper margin of the window. Skelton feels the delicate touch of navel about the end of his nose, stomach tightens in tickling and a plane of pale tan light grades away in his vision, a Venusian touch to chin whose cleft it is not, crinkling slide against cheek, then a hirsute horizon surmounting a liquid slot: Geronimo!

Birds suddenly crowd the window, slate of warblers, and scatter in a cascade of trills. On the kitchen table, a slab of cake with an emblematical mouse in black seems the calling card of some figment.

Then an easy, yielding entry and in Miranda's face baleful shadows of ecstatic misery. And Skelton, dizzy in an existence that occupies less than a single dimension, rises ultimately to that procreative fission that lights up in his darkened head like a silver tree.

Some ten minutes later, wandering to the bathroom to wash his face, he struggles for purchase on the tile floor and falls into the tub.

"Are you all right?"

"I was struggling for purchase."

"Here, let . . ."

Now she is in the tub with him. They struggle for purchase against the porcelain. The window here is smaller and interferes not at all with the smoky swoon of half-discovered girls in which Skelton finds himself. In his mind, he hears *Lovesick Blues* on the violin. He reaches for a grip and pulls down the shower curtain, collapses under embossed plastic unicorns. The shaft of afternoon light from the small window misses in its trajectory the tub by far; the tub is in the dark; the light ignites a place in the hallway, a giant shining a flashlight into the house. A rolled copy of the *Key West Citizen* hits the front porch and sounds like a tennis ball served, the first shot of a volley . . . Traffic bubbles the air. Skelton thinks that what he'd like is a True Heart to go to heaven with.

JAMES POWELL SAID, "YOUR GRANDFATHER stopped payment on that check. I had to cover all that three-quarter marine out of my own pocket; I think I'm even took for that goddamn hull." Sure enough; there was the hull, crisp and rough-edged but exquisite as a seashell, a nautilus. Seems the old bastard would have to be throttled and flung into the cistern with his spent safes. Can't appear to get depressed about it. Maybe Bella Knowles would get her Household Current after all. False teeth sailing over Key West roofs.

"Let me track this down, James. I'll see that it's covered."

Powell was sore, using that expression of angry wonder at the cupidity of others that is an impossible emotion to sustain legitimately and which therefore bears always the sweet incense of fraud. "I called old Nichol Dance to tell him I was ready to make him a boat. But the bloody bugger has gone to Islamorada to buy one, so I'm afraid you and your cheap-ass old granddad has about cooked my goose!"

"Now James, like I told you, this here is going to be covered, unless you tell me to forget all about it."

"No, I ain't saying that! I'm just saying it gets old when you have a runaround like this. I'm too busy for no runaround! *And it just gets old!*"

"I know what you mean; but look here, you get on with it now and build that skiff because I will make sure you have every cent of your money. Now you do know that, don't you?"

"WHAT TIME IS IT?"

"Six."

"You want to stop by my folks' house with me?"

"Sure, okay."

"I have got to get this skiff. I'm getting on in years."

Miranda said without challenge, "I wish I could understand."

"It's the only thing I can do half right. It's as simple as that."

"What about biology? Your old teachers told me you were gifted."

"They said that? Huh. Well, yes I was good at it. But it needn't have taken me that many years of school to see I just liked salt water, you know, at some really simple phenomenological level. I like fishing better than ichthyology because it's all pointless and intuitive. I mean, there is no value equivalent in biology for the particular combination of noise and sight of blackfin tuna working bait in the Gulf Stream. Have you ever eaten in there?"

"The Fourth of July? No. I usually go to the O.K."

"Good crawfish enchilada and good flan with you know, like caramel on the bottom. My grandfather got shot by a Cuban in that parking lot twenty years ago. Survived."

Navy personnel drove past in a staff car, craning around to see Miranda quite obviously not wearing anything under her shift: seventh-grade boys diving for the chalk, Commander Merkin of the carrier escort vessel *Invincible* wrenching his neck in a flash daydream of how quickly he'd give up the Annapoline idyl of water murder for a crack at deploying polliwogs through his bosun's whistle into the cushy little bomb bay that young lady doubtless had concealed on her person. Rushing on to base headquarters, he raised manicured fingertips to his sore neck and cleared his mind of bilge.

Skelton thought for a minute about telling Miranda of Nichol Dance; he had hinted of his utopianist scheming as to fishing; it might be honest to add this. A man passed in a sandwich board; the Paraclete's visage on the front, the word NOW on the back; brain raid of street-side cryptograms.

"A man has told me if I guide he'll shoot me."

"*What?*"

"Well, yes that."

The superimposition of violence to pointless sport caused Skelton to feel a mild creeping of the cerebellum: fistfights over golf putts, tennis buffs kicking each other in the shins with steel-toe industrial safety shoes, ping-pong kamikaze maniacs slashing at enemies' faces with reddish paddles, skeet shooters peppering schoolgirls with birdshot, chess masters quietly decoding the brains of adversaries: all contrived to make the riverboat gambler of the nineteenth century with a Philadelphia cap-and-ball .41 caliber derringer on a hide string hanging behind his lace-front shirt playing everything-wild, one-eyed-jacks, king-with-the-ax, fours-and-whores type poker seem *altogether on the up and up!*

"I like the idea of living behind a wall in this noisy town," Miranda said. Skelton pushed open the gate, a cabinet of greenery, speeding lizards, a bird screaming in the soursop tree, the Da Vincian geometry of unpruned oleander.

"Think *House of Seven Gables* and you will have fun here; it's just a little American home in another time warp."

Immediately through the gate, they could see Skelton's mother and grandfather, standing off to one side at the kitchen entrance, abruptly gesturing to them to come; quite evidently indicating that they would have to sneak by the gauze-enclosed bed, solitary as an island on the broad green-and-white porch.

"Miranda this is my mother."

"Hello, Miranda," said his mother, smiling enough to make inscrutable slits of her eyes; but Skelton saw the examining flicker.

"And my grandfather." Skelton's grandfather caught one of Miranda's hands in both of his as you would catch a small creature so that you could lift your upper hand carefully and perceive the creature peering out at you. And bent over her, a chicken over a piece of corn. "Thomas," said his mother, "your father had some kind of a fit. He has got the idea that if you guide, someone will kill you—"

"Imagine." Skelton cast a cautioning glance at Miranda.

"—and he made your grandfather cancel that check."

"Yeah, I found out."

"Don't worry about it," his grandfather said, "that part is easy to straighten out."

"The question is, where does he get such a notion."

"I couldn't guess," said Skelton.

"Well, we can," said his grandfather.

"He is out on the town now every night," said his mother, "where he is privy to all the gossip and foolishness available in Key West—"

"What he is doing, where he is going," said his grandfather in the tone of Philbrick of *I Led Three Lives*, "none of us can say. But he is at large and I don't like it."

"I thought you wanted him to get out of bed so bad."

"Not like this, Tom. Not like a sneak a . . . a figure of the night, Tom."

"A figure of the night . . . !"

"We had this from him during the war," said his mother. "He went to Fort Benning . . ." She trailed off suddenly, looking almost angrily into space. Could she have only now remembered.

"Your mother is absolutely right. He was around here like an I don't know what. He was arrested for sword fighting! Hung out with criminals! The worst of it I can hardly tell."

"*Who cares!*" said his mother. "Tell him the whole thing."

"There was a house of ill repute."

"What about it?" Skelton said.

"It was his, lock, stock, and whores." His mother looked away at this last. His grandfather studied her. "Uh, ladies of fortune."

Skelton looked at Miranda. He had only known about the whorehouse for twenty years. Why did they need to tell Miranda?

"A real one?" he asked his grandfather; let them have their fun.

"Not really," his grandfather smiled condescendingly; there was an inadvertence in the expertise he implied. "It was just an old falling-down conch house with half a dozen highfliers from Miami." He looked at his daughter-in-law and winked. "Even they couldn't take him. He had a hootchy-cootchy from Opa-Locka. Even she thought he was dumb!"

"You know, fake air raids. Fire drills where he ran from room to room hosing down his own customers," said Mrs. Skelton.

"It was ridiculous. Pictures of Jim Thorpe on the walls. The Boy Scout Oath. The Constitution. An anarchist library in the front room. Statues of saints. A clothing-store dummy dressed as the Pope. I mean, God. What kind of whorehouse . . . ! He carried things too far. Seltzer bottles. Custard pies. No one goes to a whorehouse for that! They can stay home and watch the Three Stooges. And the girls got tired of it the minute the pies started flying. They always had colds from the Seltzer. It was ridiculous."

"Running guns," said his mother in a drone. "And you're right about the colds."

"Yes, yes," said his grandfather. "Shrimping!"

"Drove a taxi. The only thing he didn't think of—"

"*Was guiding*," Skelton and his grandfather inter-rupted simultaneously.

"Go on now," said his mother, "wake him up. It's time."

Skelton crossed the porch and juggled the squeaking cedar mosquito frame, thinking about revealing to his father that everyone knew he was a figure of the night. He decided not to because it would not be interesting to do so.

"I'm awake."

"Hello, Dad. This is Miranda."

"How do you do, Miranda."

"Hello."

"What are they telling you over there?"

"Nothing much."

"About my whorehouse, weren't they?"

"Yes."

"It was a beacon of sanity. Pairing off in the most ceremonial way, unexpected friendship and disease, field-hospital camaraderie, orgasms. Miranda," said his father, "have you ever been a prostitute?"

"No, I haven't."

"You'd make a dandy."

"Thank you."

"I'm pleased you take it as a compliment. Dear ones have come to me from whoring. It's a modus operandi I understand very well."

"None of us have had good sense," said Skelton, "except my mother and we're all beginning to bore her."

"Is that a violin you have in there, Mr. Skelton?" asked Miranda.

"Yes, it is."

"Would you play something?"

"I don't know how. From time to time it plays itself and I attach myself to its moving parts. Now it sleeps lightly, twitching like a dog."

SOMETIMES WHEN A WINO COMES OFF A BAT he is as unmanageable from this grape residue in his "system" as he would be with semi-fatal dumdum rounds in the brain pan; he is, moreover, spavined in the morals. If he is in a neighborhood, he looks darkly about himself at his neighbors. A dire grape madness is upon him; and not the Castalian libido Olympiad of the wine's first onslaught that ends with an alpha-wave glissando into sleep; from which he has every expectation of waking in other than this Wild Kingdom Mutual of Omaha rhino rush, smashing of beak and noggin against the Land Rover of life itself. Especially not if the wine is one of the chemical daydreams of the republic's leisure-time industrial combines that produce and bottle curious, opaque effluents in the colors of Micronesian tides or meteor trails; these things are called "beverages" and exist not only in their bright fruit-festooned bottles but conceptually in the notebooks of technicians, diagrams of hydrocarbon chains that can be microfilmed if another "winery" should be after their secrets. It is, you suppose, one of the troubles we are having with our republic.

Such a wino had abandoned himself upon the interior of Skelton's fuselage. Skelton found him asleep in a bed of his own trashing. He woke the man up. The wino, whose delicately intelligent face was that of an amateur translator or local begonia prince, looked about himself at the wreckage and asked, "Did I do this?" cringing for the first of the blows.

"It appears that you did."

Long quiet.

"What are you going to do."

"I'm going to clean it up," said Skelton.

"I mean what are you going to do to me?"

"I'm going to be disappointed in you."

"How can you be disappointed in me? You had no expectations."

This stumped Skelton for a moment. "I have expectations about humanity in general," he finally said.

"Please, why don't you come off it. I'm a sick-ass drunk and I don't need that kind of romance."

"What do you want?"

"I want nothing. But I want plenty of nothing."

"Well, let me tell you as proprietor of this place what I got in mind. First I'm going to roll your sorry hide into the roadway so that I can clean up your damn wreckage."

"That's more like it. We are in extremis here, chum. And it's time for a dialogue."

"I don't want it—"

"It's time for polemics."

"—You wrecked my home."

"Precisely."

For Skelton, this brought back terrible memories of school. He looked about himself and thought, Why did this interlude seek me out?

NICHOL DANCE RAN HIS SKIFF DOWN THE trailer's rollers over the edge of the ramp and hand-walked it around to his slip and tied it; it was a skiff so old it had Cuban hardwood gunwales. *One thing no one could ever make me do*, thought Dance, *is start over. I would listen to all the resurrection plans anyone had for me. But starting over is out of the question*. He looked at the skiff and thought, *I am lucky that miserable gunk-board floats.*

Saturday night. By Carter's good offices, the Chamber of Commerce as part of its touristic activities had bought a day's guiding from Dance; and it was being awarded as a contest prize tonight down at Mallory Square.

They asked that Dance show up to hand the winner a certificate entitling him to the day's fishing.

THERE WERE TWENTY OF THEM LINED UP OUT front, seated behind the long wooden table. Officials stood at either end holding stop watches and counting devices. Mallory Square was full of the laughing, the hooting, and the damaged of brain; Ohioans who wore hats they had used to hold chicken eggs all winter were gathered in knots and clusters. Californians with rakish sideburns moved with cosmopolitan aplomb. The Kounter Kulture was everywhere, rolling its eyes, fingering costly jewelry. In a few minutes out here, it was going to be the republic.

Nearby, the big catering trucks were assembled, their internal steam tables giving off a moist warmth even outside the trucks, even in all this muggy weather.

Dance had been drinking a little Lem Motlow Number Seven; and he watched anxiously, mentally sizing up the twenty from all over America, trying to think which one would be confined with him in the skiff. No one, it seemed, could overlook the tall, raw-boned redhaired man who dominated the far end of the table. He was from Montana and his name was Olie Slatt. His speech introducing himself, as all the contestants had to, was the most interesting:

"*I am Olie Slatt. And don't you ever forget it. I*

mine for subbituminous low-sulphur coal in the Bull Mountains of Roundup, Montana, where they have to blast through twenty feet of sandstone to reach the vein. We have two spoils banks with eight slopes and four different strata arrangements. I'm damned proud of that and I'm going to win today. Don't you ever forget it."

Olie Slatt had a constituency in the audience and they yelled, "Mother dog! Mother dog!" with ardor.

There were others more prepossessing, to be sure, even to Nichol Dance; but none with the immensely formidable, almost insect-like jaws of this redhead.

All three of the women sat together; no one could say how they would do but everyone sensed that the aggregate result would be impressive; they consulted among themselves, these women, as if they meant to work as a team.

Nichol Dance had the certificate and shifted it from hand to hand to keep from spoiling it with sweat.

Before he was really prepared for the event, it was upon him. Abruptly, uniformed men from the truck were trooping to the tables, tall piles of stacked pies in their hands. By the time the pies were emplaced, with the flavor choices of the contestants honored, the judges had raised their pistols.

Then the guns were fired and all twenty lashed into the pies; a moment later and the slowest contestants had eaten five; and in another moment, the first vomiter rose, the gelatinous, undigested cherries of her "flavor option" dribbling down her chest.

And very quickly it was over. Losers were roughly hustled away from the table and the redhead was left alone. He looked around himself in happy disbelief for the brief remaining moment before he was declared the winner. Then all hesitation vanishing, he rose powerfully, baying his triumph in an impressive hurricane of crumbs, the insect jaws agape.

When Nichol Dance gave him his certificate, he said, "Boy, fishing is all I'm about! I'm the mother dog of all fishermen and I want to go out with you real bad—" With the word "bad" he began to vomit all over himself.

And Dance went off in a panic, saying, "Well, I'll look to hear from you down to the dock. *I hope you're feeling better!*"

"Look, in the brown shirt and the heavy tan, see him? He's starting to leave now—"

"I see him, I see him!" said Miranda. "That's the first killer I have ever seen. Does he have a notch on his pistol?"

"He may have one."

"Well, I think he ought to be in jail."

"He is, a good deal of the time."

"Don't you hate him?"

"I admire him. There is nothing like feeling your days may be numbered. Everybody's days are numbered but because of him I know it more surely even though I might live to be a hundred. This afternoon I had five orgasms, which would have been impossible if there hadn't been someone in town who wanted my life."

"Would you rather number your days or your orgasms?" asked Miranda.

"Does it come with the dinner?"

"The only thing that comes with the dinner now is progress. The rest is à la carte. What would you recommend?"

Clever girl, thought Skelton, I must show flash: "The *spécialité de la maison*, depending on the night, is whooping crane with blanched almonds or various fricassees of endangered species with *pommes frites*. For a consideration, the headwaiter can arrange to have your table bulldozed while you dine; and, I might add, on Saturday evenings a tour of the kitchens is available, where all of the cooking is by controlled napalm flash, you know, with Baked Alaska à la Dow and, natch, side orders are always available of gook-in-his-own-juices, which is nothing so much like the *calamares en su tinta* of the Basques; for the salad lover, a defoliation buffet is continually in operation!"

"My mouth is watering."

Truth is, Skelton was wound up like a cuckoo clock; and the frenetic glibness of the kind he just trotted out for Miranda was something he had long meant to avoid. Maybe Dance was doing it to him.

He could no longer synthesize the life of his father, his grandfather, and himself; he realized now, however, that that was something he had been trying to do all along. It was all coming up, but nothing in sequence.

MIRANDA TOOK HIM TO SEE FRIENDS OF HERS who lived on Petronia. Dopers. Skelton watched them, two men and a woman, as they waltzed gaga around the room to do walkie-talkie gags on the telephone with vague roots in ordering Chinese food or pizzas. A hookah burned on the floor and the proprietor of the house, a harmless witling in a jellaba, broke out his collection of "drips" for Skelton's delectation.

He placed a cardboard shoe box at Skelton's feet; it contained minutely scissored photographs of water drips sliding down cans and bottles in advertisements.

"Toughest part of commercial art, making those drips run down a bottle or can in a way that looks right to the camera. You have to wet down the whole fuckin thing, then make a track for the drip with a toothpick. Then you start the drip at the top of the bottle or whatever and when she starts to get up speed you flash your picture. You go through thousands of toothpicks looking for a good one. It—is—a—killer!"

Skelton looked into the shoe box: a hundred thousand drips—a whole culture in parable. These people couldn't save him.

"I'M SORRY TO COME SO LATE; CAN YOU GIVE me a dozen live shrimp?"

With Miranda on Geiger Key, at Marvin's bait camp; when you called on old Marvin at an odd hour he usually told you it was just as well; because this time next year he would be in hell. He was a witty man of orthodox religion, and saw his coming perdition as a malicious joke of primarily comic value. With twenty of his early years in an Appalachian mine, he had black lung and wheezed around the dock toting his bait net.

Marvin dipped the shrimp by flashlight into Skelton's bucket; they shot about backward, their ruby eyes shining.

"I hear you're gonna guide," said Marvin; he was half shaved and his Cuban wife was peering out from their house, which floated at the end of an unfixed dock upon navy oil drums.

"Inside the month. Who told you?"

"Jamesie Powell. You gonna permit fish?"

"That's how I mean to make my reputation."

"Want me to save you bait crabs?"

"I wish you would. Dollar-size."

"Want some chum crabs?"

"I'm going to pole."

"Hard guy," he said.

Skelton was running the wooden wreck he learned the country in under a sky clouded with stars. The water was black in the night, the mangrove keys blacker, and the boat smelled of uncured sponges and unretrieved fragments of bait; it smelled bad. Miranda was in front; Skelton thought he could see her.

"How can you tell where you are going?"

"Vision."

The Scott-Atwater engine cried like a baby on the transom; it had repeatedly tried to throw in the towel since Eisenhower's first administration. A gibbous and Olympic moon breasted the clouds meter upon meter. Skelton checked the shrimp with the flashlight; eyes still brilliant, they hovered like birds instead of darting against the sides of the bucket.

Now nearing Cayo Agua, he slowed down and finally coasted in alongside the mangroves, shutting off the engine. At first there was silence and then the reedy conversation of birds from the interior of the key. When the boat was at rest, the moon began to penetrate the clear water and fish could be seen glistening and gliding among the mangrove roots. The breeze barely moved enough to be felt; but the key sighed like the souls in purgatory.

Miranda said, "One of us say something philosophical."

"Miranda, we're on the ocean meadow far far from the laughing kangaroos of the F.A.O. Schwarz mainfloor toy room. This will do more to save you than either religion, futurism, or the pecky cypress walls of your West Marin hideaway."

Skelton threaded a kicking shrimp onto Miranda's

hook and instructed her to cast; which she did with evidence of having done it before. He thought: facetiousness can be a way of dancing at the edges of the beautiful; it can also be facetiousness.

"Miranda honey, look here: all of us"—he gestured around the boat—"are just free people looking to be prisoners, hoping for a quiet cell, a toothbrush and a washcloth; but we are the convicts of freedom. We look up with stony eyes from our old road-gang lives at all the vacationers we think we see heading for Tenerife, Leningrad, and the Mermaid Show at Weekeewatchee Springs. Miranda, life can become a refrigerator brimful of chilled wet hair. Or not."

"In a certain light," Miranda said, "you can see anything at all." That was deft.

More to the point, Miranda caught a mangrove snapper which made a gentle thunder on the boat bottom; Skelton sapped it once with a carriage bolt, rebaited Miranda's hook; then with the flashlight tucked under his chin, he promptly filleted the snapper and laid the pearly meat on one end of a strip of brown paper and rolled it once. Miranda kept catching snappers and when they had six pairs of fillets they quit and poured the remaining bait over the side. Brilliant fish raced in the moonlight beneath them, catching the shrimp.

The wind had nearly ceased entirely; and the few clouds left had consolidated into a single continent to the west so thin the stars showed behind its edges. The night seemed ruptured on a gloating moon.

Skelton pulled the starter through once and the engine coughed into a marginal operative existence, bebopping on the transom giddily. Skelton stood up taking the broom-handle tiller and headed for Key West glowing to the east of them pale as an aurora.

Twenty minutes of this night running and they

were close enough to home that they could see a Greyhound bus cross the Stock Island bridge and penetrate
the zygote of Cayo Hueso. Just beyond, the drive-in
theater screen loomed among the trailers. Skelton
stared: Appomattox Courthouse; Yankees and Rebels
stately in the Key West sky. From the seaward vantage,
it was the America you weep for. Ulysses S. Grant and
Robert E. Lee knee-deep in mobile homes surrounded
by the vacant sea. Lee's horse, Traveller, materialized
and vanished in the Atlantic skyway. Then Grant took
Lee's hand and it was one nation indivisible; horses,
heroes, tents, and munitions sunk among the mobile
homes: THE END.

They stopped at a package store on the way to the
fuselage and picked up a six-pack of Budweiser. It was
a pleasant store and Tennessee Williams's picture was
on the wall; the playwright was holding a whitish bull-
dog and smiling without guile.

Entering the fuselage, Skelton decided that if he
ever had some fame, he would offer his portrait to the
wino hotel, where it would be hung in the front hall out
of the reach of angry hands and flung bottles.

Skelton cut the snapper into fingers and deep fried
them in oil so hot it was just between smoking and beginning to speckle; the delectable fish sealed quickly.
He put it all in a paper-lined basket and set it on the table
with the six-pack, a pot of tartar sauce, and quartered
limes from his own tree. Then they ate like there was no
tomorrow. Plus one quickie, dog-style.

It was a school night; and Miranda went home on
her bicycle. An hour later, Skelton's phone rang. It was
Miranda.

"Tom, your father was here."

"Go on."

"He was wearing a sheet sort of pinned around him,

you know, like a Roman . . . He was hopping around like a maniac . . ."

"Tell me the rest." Doom.

"He wanted a date."

GOD WHAT A TIME. SUCH A LOSS OF FAITH THE Annunciation seemed an indecent advance. Everybody who had opened his eyes had been to hell and gone before he half knew it.

Thomas Skelton's mind had been reduced, as a fractured limb is reduced. Everyone looked at this improvement and remarked, "What a waste," or words to the effect.

Skelton looked all about himself and thought, *I need for something to come in handy real bad. Boy, that sure would be good.*

By dint of sloth, nothing had set in. And Skelton had been swept along. The cue ball of absurdity had touched the billiard balls in his mind and everything burst away from the center. Now the balls were back in the rack. Everyone should know what it is to be demoralized just so everyone knows what it is to be demoralized.

The king's ransom, the dog in the manger, the cat that swallowed the cream . . . A potato-like president, limp with murder, turns to his piquant attorney general and says, "I'd give America for a thirteen-year-old nympho." But the attorney general always replies, "No soap." Always.

Before you know it, it's a month of Sundays and you're a goner. Do remember that. The trick is to be all smiles. To be uncalled for. If you're at one remove, you're already too far gone.

Every night on TV: America con carne. And eternity is little more than an inkling, a dampness . . . Even simple pleasure! The dream of simultaneous orgasm is just a herring dying on a mirror.

THE MORNING RITUAL OF DRESSING, REDOLENT of an implicit dandyism, began after icy water returned the features to Skelton's face. He paused always at the mirror in those precious moments before full awakening to see an utterly amoral creature, slack as a murderer; and thought of the serenity of Starkweather before his accusers. Then cold water, and a sharpness returned; a fellow creature began to form like a mirage over his features; a creature who could compete elbow to elbow with anyone and who would fistfight shrimp captains over principles not even believed. Then well-broken Levi's sun-bleached and long, a braided leather belt, and a Cuban guayabera shirt that had already made its deal with the heat. When Skelton stood up after lacing his deck shoes, he wanted to feel his weight settle just slightly toward the heels; and when his spirits were particularly high, it seemed there was a full four feet between his belt buckle and his chin. At such times, he felt his movement was like a compass needle swinging inexorably and at a sweep, drawn rather than pushed.

Too often, he woke up miserable, wanting to stand in a slump, one eye needing to go one way, the other another. He felt the ridges between his eyebrows deepen and he could stand a good antacid, a Rolaid for example, or an Alka-Seltzer; even a gay, foaming all-American Bromo would have been, you know, *terrific*. In such a mood, Skelton was Starkweather howled at by his girlfriend's parents for using their car; and for being a garbage man in Lincoln, Nebraska, where teenagers learn the Australian crawl at sun-drenched, cretinoid country clubs, where even aging wage slaves burn up the Cornhuskers Highway on polyglas radial tires; the American Plains in a blue rear-view mirror; and slender green traffic islands penetrating the steppes and old treeless, buffalo-haunted dreamland of a vacant republic.

It must have been something Skelton ate.

Sometimes the buzz of a housefly in an empty room has the timbre of the human voice. On moonless nights, simple cities of the Plains bear witness to strange events: an elderly drunk charges over celery terraces, baying, "Peaceniks have fobbed off with my daughter!" And somewhere in the Dakotas, a hunter's lost beagle passes the night chewing the main cable of the President's Hot Line. When he leaps back, his head a blue spark, he gives a single bark and is gone; separated by continents and oceans, a commissar and a president run to headquarters in their pajamas. There you have it.

These were heavy thoughts and Skelton sat down. He knew that the word "serious" does not derive from the word "cereal." He had a feeling that on the Plains of America everyone was named Don and Stacy. He knew that spiritual miniaturism frequently lay waiting in the foothills where a ranch was exchanged for a golf course; and that the Spalding Dot, the Maxfli, and the Acushnet soared over the bones of dead warriors. So, if he were driven from Key West, he knew the Plains were not the place he'd go.

Skelton wandered around the fuselage. Don and Stacy had come to life on the American Plains. It was the frontier and Don threw a glass of Lavoris in Stacy's face. It was the end of something. Stacy direct-dialed Mom at Leisureland, demanding a one-way on the jumbo jet. This was enough. Number-one son, Lance, caught a Cong mortar in the mouth in Nam. Daughter Sherri cold-turkeyed in the Oregon Women's Detention Center, then divorced her Gypsy Joker husband to marry a Young American for Freedom. The Young American for Freedom liked to put birthday candles up her behind, eat confetti, and spray Welch's grape juice on her thighs. At night, Don would sit before the freestone fireplace in the rec room, read his social security card, and harp. Stacy made spitballs in the storm cellar. Is it any wonder they woke up plumb grousing?

Skelton was in a bad mood. The morning ritual, with dandyism, hadn't cured it. He isolated his troubles to two specific areas: his father's show at Miranda's the night before and Nichol Dance's promise. He would see both of them today; the air was beginning to acquire the opacity again that it had before he clarified his life; now he had to do it again. It was, he thought for the moment, a case of bailing a leaky boat. But, well, do it.

SKELTON'S GRANDFATHER, THE REDOUBTABLE, with, out of his long years on earth, not a day in the service of his country, remembered the wars from his sea-level eyrie in Cayo Hueso.

During the glum scheming of the First War, when Thomas Edison had experimented with depth charges at navy headquarters on Key West, Goldsboro kept a cruiser at Garrison Bight for the express purpose of whoremongering and trips to Cuba of mysterious object.

One war later, his son, Skelton's father, kept a converted rum-runner as a fishing launch with the black flag of anarchism flying from its transom. Dizzily evading all known goals, he had become a chimera.

Now here is what Skelton wondered: was there a connection between himself and these two male forebears? And if there was, what was he being steered toward? Universal consciousness or early death? And lastly, why did both seem oceanic? He could not escape the suspicion that this association of boats—cruiser, rum-runner, skiff—implied something sequential. He feared that if he could go back one more generation on hard data to his great-grandfather, he would discover the old wrecking master in the maze of his schooner's cordage running the southerly shoals, spaced-out and as incipiently suicidal as fifty 1947 Existentialists.

G. Skelton himself, meanwhile, moved through his safe-cluttered offices. Safes of every vintage, opened, closed, dynamited, doorless or lock-picked, seemed a kind of audience for the streams of thought that poured uninterrupted from a brow as round and serene as a radar dome.

If there was a single thing for which he had a gift, besides that of pulling rugs out from under his opponents, it was for a kind of manipulation of conditions so that the problem or the solution seemed fresh to the point of being raw. He had for example, carefully kept his grandson dancing on a string of unease over this guide boat. On the one hand, he wanted it to be as vivid as only uncertainty could make it; and, on the other, he could not resist the dicey gaming around, the spirals of manipulation that were the actual texture of his life. When Goldsboro Skelton walked around his bailiwick and viewed his contemporaries sunning away their last days on earth in louvered porches, he thanked Christ for the grandiose instinct for creating a vortex that had been his since the turn of the twentieth century.

Goldsboro Skelton had been among the last Key Westers to go to sea with the wrecking masters before he was twenty, had piloted a diesel ferry that had been built a hundred forty miles up the Mississippi through the impossible Delta and across the Gulf of Mexico in offshore summer storms, a vessel of minimal sheltered-water freeboard never designed for such open-sea crossings. He was religiously ambiguous—"I deal with Jesus directly"—and had acquired some fame on a salvage trip in his teens with a dipsomaniacal wrecking master who kept the young Goldsboro Skelton and six school friends in the superheated hold of a condemned freighter that had broken its back on a Honduran reef a hundred miles out of Stann Creek; seven youths loading crude sugar from the steaming hold of a boat that creaked and shifted on the reef and threatened to roll with their lives inside. When the freighter groaned more than usual or when the slow scream of its iron hull against the implacable coral rose a quarter octave, Skelton and the others would plead to go topsides in case the freighter should finally roll. But the wrecking master, who often knelt on the salvage boat bobbing safely alongside to pray Jaheezuss for the safety of those young souls, his hands and eyes fluttering firmament-ward in a curiously female explosion of emotion, the wrecking master always said quite emphatically, no. Then on the third day of salvage, a jet of blue Caribbean came in through the packing seal around the shaft, a blast of sea water that looked vividly like the end, jetting out across tons of unrefined sugar in the heat.

This time, Skelton fetched himself a seven-pound splinter from the fractured oak stringers of the sugar freighter and carried it to where he found the wrecking master praying in the shade of the pilothouse. He took the good captain off his knees with the first blow of that scantling across his god-fearing fundament; then marched him to the forecastle where he was confined to quarters with all the green-glass shippers' demijohns of bad Cuban rum he could drink. By now Skelton's terrified shipmates were there to hear a speech that became the rooftree of his early fame.

"I am now the master of this vessel," he said more magisterial than would seem possible. "And you are forbidden to pray."

A week later, Goldsboro Skelton was tried and acquitted of mutiny. The first strands of his net had begun to spin out over Key West. He was a hero of the streets.

"BELLA, BELLA, BELLA," GOLDSBORO SAID, TOO weary to mount the trampoline.

"All right."

"I'm mean, you know."

"Tired."

"Well, yes, tired; but no tireder than you, Bella. I just won't pretend like you will pretend, busting your butt till the cows come home just to prove that time doesn't pass."

"No, Goldsboro, I'm not tired. You're tired. I'm not tired. But you honey, you're real tired."

"Could you still sing, Bella?"

Bella Knowles had twice performed at the World of Disney Planetarium, actually before that place had been constructed; but the dreams and romance of those intrepid Americans had led them to at least put up the visitors' center, little more than a Quonset hut in the sodden alligator marsh; and a giant styrene figment of Donald Duck.

"I could still shatter glass with my voice, e.g., my vitality."

Goldsboro Skelton, less La Manchan than Cartesian, ran out of the gym and returned with a fine wineglass.

"Where do you want it?"

"Anywhere. Right there. Go on, on the table."

Bella Knowles prepared her lungs, breathing deeply and composing her face in a deep abstracted expression, like a policeman suddenly confronted with a problem in jurisprudence. Suddenly she screamed at the glass.

Nothing. She screamed again. Nothing.

"I can only do it when I'm excited."

"Oh no you don't. I told you: tired."

"Then I can't smash the glass."

"You couldn't anyway."

"I could if I were excited."

"What if we did the mop."

"I could smash the glass."

He went into the next room, where shortly the surge of water in a pail could be heard. As he did so, Bella Knowles sat on the floor and struggled out of her girdle. Skelton returned to the room with a pail of suds and a mop. Bella Knowles knelt on all fours before the small table upon which the wineglass rested, face raised point-blank to the glass, heaving with her wind exercises.

Goldsboro Skelton's skepticism was visible as he plunged the mop into the suds and began to slop it foaming around Bella Knowles's behind. After four full and foaming minutes, she inhaled deeply and shrieked like a banshee. The glass shattered.

Abruptly, she rose to her feet, weeping silently with pride, and flung herself into her ungrateful lover's arms. She stood there a long time in a gradually enlarging puddle of suds; shards of crystal were scattered about the table. And somehow, the suds, the pail, the mop, and the crystal were "mute testimony" to a life of charisma and reversals, the tawdry and the magnifique: in short, the universal condition of total blandness decorated only here and there, like cheap raisin bread, with modern French philosophers in waterproofs.

EIGHT-THIRTY AND SKELTON WAS TRUDGING
for the dock. He would have dreaded this meeting less
if it had been just a meeting with Dance, though he
would still have dreaded it. In any case, he was now doing not what he wished to do but what he ought to do;
and getting a gentle energy return from satisfying this
minor imperative. Carter would be there, however; so
would Roy Soleil; maybe even Myron Moorhen. All the
way to the dock, Skelton was cultivating an air of reason. He did not consider this meeting to be a showdown;
which is always an encounter of meat and blades for a
hamburger reason.

Faron Carter held in his hand a forged-steel nozzle
at the end of a large-diameter black hose that trailed in
four lazy curves all the way out to a Gulf truck at whose
wheel sat a harmless footling of the oil monsters. Into a
filler pipe, Carter was directing a golden rush of gasoline that (final suspiration of vanished forests, dinosaurs,
and simple monocot meadows) soon enough would
drive bright metal billets of cam and piston to blue whir
of propeller for getting from Point A to Point B. Otherwise, the petroleum drive for hotcakes is too well
known for further elucidation; it contests munitions for
the winning turkey. One thinks of the opossum, a simple
marsupial widely known in this land is our land. When
the mother opossum is on a trip and hunger calls, she
reaches into her pouch and eats a baby 'possum; until
eventually mother opossum is alone in the American
Night with no one to call her "Mom."

"Tom," said Carter, "you been scarce as hen's teeth.
I don't know when I seen you last—"

"Last time I saw you," said Skelton, "I was laying
on the bottom of the canal over there watching you and

Roy Rogers driving around looking for me with a pistol."

"Is ah that an admission of guilt?"

"Not unless you have concealed a court recorder in that palmetto."

"Well, nice to have you around again," said Cart, real friendly. "Your granddad come to our Lions Club luncheon yesterday and he and I had a chancet to visit awhile. Your old granddad is some character! He told me how much he was looking forward to you joinin the dock down here. And so am I! So am I . . ."

"Where's Nichol at?"

"I'm over here!" Dance's voice from behind the sea wall; must be in his skiff. That was a break: the chance to talk in private.

Skelton walked across the springy Bermuda grass toward Dance; he could just see the curve of Dance's back as he bent over the engine, an oval of dark sweat in the center of the khaki shirt.

Faron Carter walked to the door of the bait shack and met Myron Moorhen, there risen from his desk at the sound of Skelton's voice; columns of figures still seemed to hang in his ovine eyes. Beneath his jackknife nose his lower lip bunched in concern around the bright teeth of a lemur.

"I'll be."

"You'll be what, Myron."

"I didn't nearly expect to see that incendiary show his face . . . !"

"I hadn't known you to run you a court of inquiry on the subject!"

"Well, now what is the policy then?"

"We don't have no policy. Nichol Dance had the policy. Nichol Dance you may just recall is the old boy lost his boat?" This last word soaring in ridicule.

"Okay, okay."

"So he has the policy."

"Okay."

"And we live and let live or die and let die whichever the case may be."

"I get it then," said Myron Moorhen. "Ours is a policy of non-intervention and Dance's is . . . is what?"

"Dry up, Myron."

Myron wandered dutiful to the numbers. The shrimp tank aerator bubbled; and the whole place smelled to high heaven because a customer had left a wahoo on the tournament scale all weekend and it had turned.

Myron Moorhen started his Bic at the top of the third column and ran it clear to the last figure; where he moved its point horizontally to the word "debit."

"What all is going to happen?"

"Someone is going to get killed," Carter replied. "Myron, where did you put that wahoo?"

"I DON'T SEE WHY A BUSTED O-RING WOULD cause the engine to quit."

"All right now," said Dance, "pay attention now." He swung the engine over to one side. "The o-ring I'm talking about is right up here at the top of the drive shaft and keeps sea water from getting up here—right?—past the crank—right?—and killing the engine."

"How did you know the o-ring was busted?"

"I figured it was, is how. Then I pulled the power-head and there it was in pieces."

"How did the rest of it look?"

"It didn't look good. I pulled the impeller in the water pump and the rubber blades were all deteriorated."

"How does it run now?"

"Go up forward and start it."

The engine turned over and caught quickly; but idled unevenly. "Not great," Skelton was the first to say.

"Run it up another thousand." The engine came up to pitch; but still rough. It was an old-timer. "Let's see how it runs. I just changed the nineteen-inch prop it had for a twenty-one."

Skelton freed the lines and sat down in the portside chair. Then Dance sat down and wheeled the boat away from the dock. It was not an unhandsome skiff, a very old Roberts made on Tavernier.

Dance said, "Lightning struck those little keys east of the Snipes day before yesterday; I have to make a quick run over there and see. There's a lot of birds out there. I want to see how did they do."

They ran directly across Jewfish and Waltz Key basins and jumped the bank behind Old Dan Mangrove because they had the tide. Skelton studied Dance handling the tricky run. He went up behind the Mud Keys and broke through to the Gulf just northwest of the Snipes and turned east, shutting down over sandy bottom so that the shadow of the boat on the bottom swung and pivoted as the wake overtook the boat. The skiff came to rest, locked to its shadow as though on a pendulum.

Skelton jacked up the engine by hand; it had no power tilt. Dance got up on the bow and poled them toward the beach in the thunderous old storm wash that came in off the Gulf. On the reef line, green rollers poured through the surge channels.

Dance threw the anchor high up on the beach; and they went ashore. Before they walked up into the beach grass they could see a couple of wild palms shattered by lightning, some with livid streaks in their smooth gray trunks. As soon as they were up on the higher part of the key, they found a number of white herons, little blue herons, and one wood stork, killed by the lightning. "Isn't that a crime," said Dance. The birds were already throbbing and heavy with worms, perhaps ten birds scattered as the lightning had found them, long wading legs crisscrossed, beaks pointing about ridiculously in this last idleness of death.

They started back. They were halfway across Waltz Key Basin before they talked again. Dance said, "Look here, I know it wasn't much of a joke."

"You're right."

"Not that it excuses what you done."

"Yeah well."

"And you cannot guide. I gave my word."

"Well, I *am* going to guide."

"You are not."

Skelton nodded that he was, as pleasant as he could.

Two spotted rays shot out in front of the boat and coursed away on spotted wings, their white ventrals showing in their hurry: then vanished in the glare. The water was still and glassy, green over the turtle-grass bottom. There were birds everywhere now, soaring out before them—the cormorants that rested on stakes and mangroves to dry out their wings, the anhingas, gulls, frigate birds, and pelicans, the wading herons and cranes of every variation of slate, whites upon whites, emblematic black chevrons or stripes, wings finished in a taper or left rough-ended. They threaded the keys amid this aerial display over uncounted fish coursing the tidal basin, over a bottom itself home to a million kinds of animal, that walked, stalked, and scuttled by every tropism from heat to light, and lived in intermeshing layers, layer upon layer, that passed through each other like light and never touched.

A jet passed over and Skelton looked up for it; every year you had to look farther ahead of the sound. The plane made a beautiful silver line.

THOMAS SKELTON FELT THAT SIMPLE SURVIVAL at one level and the prevention of psychotic lesions based upon empirical observation of the republic depended upon his being able to get out on the ocean. Solitary floating as the tide carried him off the seaward shelf was in one sense sociopathic conduct for him; not infrequently such simplicity was one of three options; the others being berserking and smoking dope all the livelong day.

Notwithstanding the shriveling of the earth before its most singular product, Skelton's reflex to be a practicing Christian remained. His skill in sidestepping confrontation, his largest capability, left him—faith, hope, and charity—largely untried. Somewhere, he knew that. It had taken a quarter of a century to produce the combination for him: access to the space of ocean (and the mode of livelihood that would make that access constant) and an unformed vision of how he ought to live on earth with others.

So he told Nichol Dance, "I am going to guide."

But today, by the time he got to Searstown, he was looking around at the human surge and thinking how attractive it must be to go shopping at the Annual White Sales without anyone offering to murder you over the percales, or to spew your guts across the Dansk Mug Set. Even the shapely teeny-bopper whom he had zero chance of having, looked in at the new Sugarcane Harris albums without the air of impending murder for *anyone*, much less herself.

And how shall I accept my own death? A forefinger

in the entrance hole while a billion protozoa redistribute my chemical components from behind where the bullet exits and kills an innocent pelican whitening a speedboat nearby.

Miranda, said Skelton to himself at Searstown, I'd feel a lot better if I could do a little barking. Imagine: The course of the bullet; its "entry" is immediately to the left of the sternum, where in its passage it disrupts the heart's determined flutter as to cause not quite immediate death. He knows what it is. There is the majesty of that surprise. His conviction that the chance against his living again is infinity minus one saves him from complete regret. Skelton's eyes, which always had a bright and fluid life, become on this sunny day quickly dry; and a place where the small insects of the empty beach can walk without . . . struggling for purchase. Gradually, his eyes become a popular trysting spot for breeding beach bugs; and by the magic geometry of mitosis, each eyeball is soon transformed into a thriving community with roots in, on the one hand, the first aeons of earth time; and, on the other, the weirdest reaches of the evolutionary space-future in which, feasibly, the products of Skelton's eyeballs might be colonizing planets of their own for reasons of civilization. By the same token, his prostate might get to the White House.

Skelton was modifying his fuselage, and shopping in the Sears hardware store for tools and parts. He bought a Craftsman variable-speed drill with a firm money-back guarantee. The magic of the electric drill was that it allowed you to take the oddly shaped hole of an electrical outlet and by running its force through a black cord and a silvery mechanism cause holes at the other end, of any size you liked.

Would Dance regret his deed? Would he look again

at that delirious passage by which what is quick and numinous becomes meat, and say: Phooey? Or would he, like the television commentators before every event, "never cease to be amazed"?

The hardware department with its bins of galvanized nails, black bolts, and chromium-plated screws, its bright power tools, was presided over by six clerks in green smocks who soared among its counters, from time to time regrouping at the cash register to clinch a sale or take a quick pull of coffee from a translucent white coffee cup. Skelton knew that—embroiled as he was as a customer—hardware, generally speaking, was bad for the world.

It was among the glues, directly behind the epoxy display, to be precise, that he knew it was time to go and see why his father was asking Miranda for a date. The two-part epoxy was best for maximum adhesion between clean flat surfaces. The one-part "mock" epoxies were "just the thing," a lady clerk volunteered, for simple household repairs, including china, furniture, butter churns, ice skates, and simple treadle assemblies.

Sweet Jesus, thought Skelton, not in the least taking the Name in vain, death is in my lane tromping the passing gear.

"Ma'am," he said to the lady clerk, whose beveled white hairdo strove implacable against air and light, "have you got time to join me in a smoke? I uh won't lay a hand on you."

She broke into laughter. Here is where Skelton could serve humanity in its gloomy mission.

"Okay."

They stood outside in the mall by speeding machines and parked-auto clusters. Skelton didn't smoke tobacco. This might be tough.

"I forgot my cigarettes."

"Have one of mine, hon." She held out a pack and he took one. A granny shot past baying on a go-cart. The gramp ran behind. He had just jerked the starter, and Gran shot off like Puffed Rice from a cannon. Now it looked like she would beat him to Akron.

"So!" said Skelton. "You smoke Luckies!"

"Two packs a day and I've tried them all."

Skelton used to smoke. He had something to say here.

"I like Camels myself."

"Well, they're a rich-type cigarette like Luckies. But Camels have I don't know too *deep* a taste for me. But I *hate* Chesterfields!"

"Me too! They're so harsh!"

"Harsh isn't the word. —Have you ever smoked filters?"

"Benson and Hedges!"

"Aha!"

"Parliaments!"

"Me too! Couldn't taste a thing! —I don't know," she said, "for me it's L.S.M.F.T., Lucky Strike Means Fine Tobacco."

Skelton pulled her into his arms. His eyes were moist. "Do you want a light?" she asked. Skelton couldn't look her in the eye.

"I really don't smoke any more."

LET US MAKE BARKING UP THE WRONG TREE A way of life.

"Your father," said his mother, "has not returned at all. He is rapidly approaching the time when he will not be allowed to return."

"Why?"

"The minute I tell, you'll say it's bourgeois."

"Is it?"

"Yes. If he decided to make of himself a figure of the night, I should have been notified."

"Why?"

"So the consequences could be negotiated. I'm leading an unnatural existence and *have been* to the point that I must now ask myself if I am to redeem any of my remaining life."

Skelton knew what she said. His father's adventures in shrimping, procurement, an ill-fated investment in a factory that would employ those of the failed cigar industry who had not moved to Ybor City in the manufacture of lighter-than-air craft purely on the somewhat mystical theory that a zeppelin and a cigar were similarly shaped—no, the Southernmost Blimp Works had not fared much better than the whorehouse; the first tropical depression and the blimps ripped up their moorings and vanished over the Gulf of Mexico. His father had been able to tolerate that; but what he resented, he said, was the whores in Duval Street cheering them on their way, his own father roaring, "Gas bags!" from the Mallory pier. The utter vanishing of the blimps, those artifacts of his father's ambitions, disturbed. Did they end up in the ionosphere? Or rip apart and sink to a lonesome sea, changing whale voices with helium bubbles? But the cry of "Gas bags!" and the door of an empty blimp works would carry through the years to a youth, his mother, a man loose in Key West streets in nothing but a bed sheet.

"Tom," said his mother, "if I only knew what he had in mind. And I know him so well. But he will do a thing . . . Oh God, I don't know. He's so contrary. He twice called off our marriage because he had a deviated septum."

"That's why he went to bed for seven months."

"And as soon as people began to count on him going to bed, he got up. Now he runs around at night. But the minute we plan on it . . . hell."

"That's all right, Mother." She was going to cry. It was like seeing Marciano cry. "Don't you think he's trying to find something?"

"I knew you would say that," she said, "it's always religion to you."

"But don't you?"

"No. I think he's contrary."

"No, you don't."

"I know I don't."

"So why do you say it?"

"Because it is impossible to understand what he could be looking for. Nonsense is nonsense."

Skelton was thinking, You could get what you want and have a laugh a minute, take a pill, see God, play a record, weep poignantly, and discover mortality on a form letter that began "Greetings." Or you could just lie there. When we came in, he was just lying there. Or you could louse up. You could fail to get the joke. You could lift up thine eyes. Skelton thought: I think I'll lift up mine eyes. When we came in, he was just lying there, his eyes at a weird angle.

His mother took her beautiful English stainless-steel pruning shears—the closest thing she had to jewelry— and began cutting back the broadleaf elephant's-ear philodendron near the stairway; these plants were rain basins that poured water onto the wooden steps, rotting them out in a year's time if they weren't pruned.

"I ask myself, should he be confined? And I always decide absolutely not. It isn't so much that he is harmless as that I have a suspicion he is on to something—"

"Me too," Skelton interrupted quickly.

"How would you know? You're just like him."

"No, I'm not."

"You're both convinced that you arrive at the right thing by eliminating all the wrong ones."

It was true. Neither he nor his father belonged to that class of succinct creatures that directly reached for what was right. The difference was that he was attracted to the merely incorrect, while his father very often began with the appalling.

"So what are you going to do about it."

His mother put her shears down.

"Nothing," she said positively. "I'm going to do nothing. Do you understand what that implies?"

THE OLD MAN, GOLDSBORO SKELTON, STOOD across from his secretary. He held a sheet of paper upon which he had written and scratched out a number of sentences.

"Okay now. Delete the sentence that ends 'unforgiven blimp fiasco.' "

"Okay . . ."

"Delete from 'cigar, mouse' all the way to 'favoring that we.' "

"Okay . . ."

"And the sentence ending 'punks and losers.' "

"Akay . . ."

"And in the whole last paragraph, cut the following words: 'duck,' 'flavor,' 'Marvin,' 'whereas,' 'celluloid,' 'bingo,' and 'dropsy.' And cut the whole song *Silver Threads among the Gold*."

"Mmmmkay, there. Darling?"

"What?"

"Take me." Bella was grimacing with amour.

Goldsboro Skelton gazed past her. A wharf rat shot

by in the foliage outside his window, scaling the trees like a squirrel. He turned to Bella Knowles.

"The big Norways are in the palm," he said.

"So?"

"So, forget the Spanish-fly act."

Bella sighed with what Skelton thought was a squalid rise of bosoms.

SKELTON MET JAMES DAVIS, SKIPPER OF THE shrimper *Marquesa*, across from the Western Union and went into Shorty's to have coffee with him. They sat at the counter, across from the great wooden cyclorama that nearly formed the wall over the stoves, and upon which a genius of the show-card school had depicted the specialties of the house. Skelton observed anew Davis's birch-stain complexion and kindly, malformed face; simultaneously Skelton noticed that the only gold inlay he himself owned had come loose.

"Not fishing today?"

"No," said James.

"How come."

"I lost my boat . . ."

"You lost your boat . . ."

"Florida First National Bank got it."

"Are you . . . working?"

"I'm the salad chef at Howard Johnson's," he said right out.

". . . I'm sorry . . ."

"Don't be."

"Well, I'm looking for my old man."

"I thought he was bedridden."

"He was."

"What happened?"

"He took a notion."

"Yeah? When?"

"Two days ago."

"Did you check with the whores?"

"I don't figure that's it."

"The priest?"

"The old man is always throwing him out."

"Maybe he's watching Triple-A. He still likes sports, don't he?"

"The World Series, pro football, and winter Olympics only. I can't figure this one out . . ."

IT TOOK AN HOUR'S WAITING TO CATCH MIranda in the schoolyard (and three blind messages by cooperative students). She came out of the study-hall door in one of the hourly blurts of humanity, a scene at the Velveeta cheese works.

"I'm so sorry," he said, referring, without need to specify, to his father's Roman appearance.

"Please, don't be concerned. I wouldn't have told you if I hadn't thought you ought to know. Then today I got something strange in the mail. I don't know if it's him again because it's unsigned." She took a manila envelope out of her folder and handed it to Skelton. Inside was an unsigned photograph.

It was a dong.

Understandably, Skelton took immediate umbrage.

"I can assure you that my father did not mail that . . . item."

"I said I didn't know it was him. And 'item' isn't quite the word."

"There is no way it could be him. It must be one of your students. And it's unsigned. And 'item' is my choice of language."

"I doubt if it's a student. Of course it's not signed! It's not a publicity photo."

"Are you being short with me?"

"Yes."

"I don't like this being attributed to my father."

"I was taking a wild guess. He was round my place in a bed sheet wanting a date."

It was easy to see how she, after refusing this figure of the night and receiving an anonymous organ photo by the morning post, might put two and two together. The former was his father all right; but until further proof was in hand, he would continue to regard the dong as a phantom.

IT LOOKED LIKE A MOTH.

Some years ago, pouring drinks in his own warm and, if he did say so, well-run tavern, listening to trainers of bird dogs, construction stiffs, and short-range drifters who straggled in out of the heat, the cold, or lack of either for a sometimes paid-for drink to talk about, generally, Sputnik, farm parity, poontang, and game-bird populations.

Among them an exercise boy of forty summers from Lexington who came every Saturday night, in costume, to drink and turn nasty. One Saturday, after Dance had cut him off at the bar, the exercise boy had waited for him to close, then beat Dance half to death in his own parking lot with a tire iron. Dressed as the Sheik of Araby, he had given Dance the curious view of a half-wit Scots-Irish face pinched murderous under the great cloud of turban as the iron came down on his head and face beyond counting.

The exercise boy vanished, eluding all known forms of law for four months; Dance recovered, though his nose, which had detached entirely and slipped up under his cheek, never did look right; not broken-looking necessarily but as though it had been picked up in a sale of another's effects.

Now one hot summer afternoon when it must have been ninety-two in the shade and the bar was empty as all get out, Nichol Dance looked up at the glaring doorway with its bands of greenery, yellow-striped road, and sky, to see the exercise boy enter as though afloat on that panel of uncomfortable light. He was dressed as a moth and wanted crème de menthe on shaved ice.

Dance told him to get out.

"Why?"

"Because I told you to. And as soon as you do go, I am going to call the law." Dance was afraid of him.

"I prefer to stay and drive you batshit," said the other, detecting Dance's fear.

"You ain't gonna drive me batshit," Dance laughed.

"Why, I already have. And I tell you what else. I got a nigger-chasin cannon in my hand I'm gone to use on your ass."

The exercise boy was sitting close enough to the bar that Dance couldn't see what he was holding. But Nichol had a gun of his own, the useful Bisley Colt with the Mexican ivory grips; and he was pointing it through the thin paneling of the bar face. The exercise boy had his right hand in his lap, smoking with his left with conspicuous awkwardness. The two talked for an endless half an hour, the exercise boy in his serpentine voice. And the first time he moved his right arm, Nichol Dance blew him halfway across the room; where he lay, all wings, and made a spot.

The law it was who discovered the exercise boy to be not armed; so Dance, unpopular enough for coming from Indiana smelling of hardware and buckeyes, was placed under arrest; it was not until his trial that he ever heard the exercise boy's name: George Washington. And Nichol Dance received a contempt citation for remarking, *What a name for that shabby-ass snake doctor.*

And now twenty-one years later in Key West, damned if there wasn't another moth-like number following him around at night. Dance cut himself one more piece of amberjack and cracked a beer. A man in his life, he thought, sure had to hack his way through a lot of lunch meat. But I will do what I have to. I'm all I've got, in a manner of speaking.

ON BIG PINE KEY, THE FIRST LIGHT OF DAY passes through the high breezy forest. A key-deer buck, the size of a dog, places four perfect scarab hoofs on Route A1A and is splattered by a Lincoln Continental four weeks out of the Ford Motor Company, carrying three admirals bound to Miami and a "kick-off breakfast" for a fund-raiser. The taillights elevate abruptly at the Pine Channel Bridge and are gone. The corporate utopia advances by a figure equal to the weight of the little buck divided by infinity; the Reckoning advances by a figure equal to the buck multiplied by infinity. A funeral wake of carrion birds, insects, and microorganisms working assiduously between bursts of traffic takes the little deer home a particle at a time.

MIRANDA WENT INTO THE BATHROOM. SHE WAS there five or ten minutes. When she came out her hair was in disarray and there were a few plastic curlers scattered arbitrarily through the snarl. She sat on the bed and began to shriek. Her face was scrubbed of all makeup; she looked like a loser in a Farm Administration photograph.

"Shittin place is drivin me nuts. You outa fuckin work and me expectin a child!"

"Honey, honey . . . I tried . . ."

"Tried my ass! You're out with faeries while I'm home wid a B-29 in the hangar!"

"A B-29 in the hangar!" Skelton fell on the floor. Miranda stared at him.

"An my ass is draggin in this shithouse while you're out golfin with flits and highfliers!"

"No more!"

"No more is right! I'm walkin outa this cockroach palace and leave you to stew in yer own juice like ya deserve ya four-bit louse!"

"Now just wait a goddamn minute. Whose a one around here with the diploma?"

"I'll tell you what I about had enough of," she shrieked, "and that's midnight visits from in-laws in sheets and weenie pictures in the mail! That's what I'm tired of!"

A knock on the door. Miranda answered it. Skelton listened from the closet. It was a neighbor. Miranda was telling her yes she was all right; they were doing psychotherapy. Not to be interrupted or the AMA would be alerted.

WHEN HER FRIENDS WERE NOT ON THE PHONE asking for advice, when no meals were to be made, when unbeset by that complicated skein of petty social contrivances in Key West to which she had many years ago been coopted as a kind of servomechanism and without which the game would have been more carnivorous than it was because she, to a degree almost no longer rememberable in our time, was a generous creature; when all that presented a clear and silent lacuna in her existence as wife, mother, and daughter-in-law to three men of the same surname and in some ways uninterrupted stripe, she retreated to the bedroom and cried quite silently, not a single sob, but just a steady, streaming exhaustion with men who had become figments of their own imaginations; and of whom she probably ought long since to have been shut. After that, she had a system of restoration: a napkin in ice water to clear the eyes, then instead of her usual subdued lipstick she applied Fire and Ice, which was precisely the color of the bright oxygenated blood of an animal mortally shot through the lungs (Skelton's imaginary death wound would have produced this color), and some rouge to highlight her prominent cheekbones (her navy officer, Oklahoma grandfather had Indian blood, of which he was not proud).

She was less mortified than demoralized by her husband's latest absurdity. Mortification ended with his army discharge and his public announcement, long after Key West knew he was home on "a mental," that Adolf Hitler was an invention of the Miami Press Club. He of course believed no such thing; but argued that it opened a useful avenue of thought. His pitiful belief in selective stupidity amid a situation of universal stupidity made it impossible for him to start anyone even daydreaming about his theories by which good guys in a monstrously linear and Ptolemaic universe demanded bad guys for the far seat of the seesaw. It was an easy idea, like those of Darwin, Francis Bacon, and Jack the Ripper.

So it all dribbled away to the point of his bedriddence; and expressed itself now in his love of running-backs who could run a slant off tackle and end up getting thirteen yards in a sweep. He believed in *lateral moves at the line of scrimmage*. She could understand that, however brittle the parallel; and it was her problem to discover now in what sense his vanishing into the darkness was a lateral move.

WHEN FARON CARTER WAS WITH HIS WIFE, HE could contrive to deprive his face of all expression whatsoever. In this way he was able to keep from letting her know where she was picking up points and where she was losing them. It was a good little stunt; and without it, Carter would doubtless be in the rubber room at the state funny farm conducting Chinese fire drills. Now, when he had deprived his face of emotion, he had a wide and expressionless mouth like the juncture of a casserole dish with its lid.

Today his wife was ironing in front of the set, watching a teenage dance hour. The music was coughing so explosively that he could feel it in the ironing board when he rested his hand. And now and then the television would give them close-ups of the dancers with the points of their tongues protruding from the corners of their mouths. It was out of this world.

Jeannie Carter had been a pretty Orlando baton twirler twenty years ago; but now she looked like death warmed over; you had the feeling that if you touched your fingernail to her forehead, the skull within would jump into your lap. She was a driven lady with the baton and back-seat feel-ups so long past they were scarcely good for an off-color laugh on pinochle night; Jeannie Carter just needed a lot of goods to keep the mortal wolf from the door. She was a forlorn little sociopath, crazy with accumulated purchases, who could have been saved from her shopping sprees only by a weekly gang-fuck behind the high school; for she was not so degenerated that the varsity club wouldn't line up the way they would, in mountain regions say, for a healthy sheep or yearling cow full of burdock and thistles. The truth was, Faron Carter did his best; but when she scrabbled, eyes popping, on his spacious chest, twisting a fierce and cosmically insatiable twat around his simple meat, it was in a vision of bleak and endless space that could only be modified to something in which she could live by purchases and then more purchases.

Now that is not to say she used her scattered ownerships to harm her neighbors, nor even, God knew, to characterize herself with her friends and what was left of her family.

It started with the showpieces. Their first showpiece was this modest concrete block house with its two bedrooms, its terrazzo-floored john and Florida room. There were reproductions on the walls that were more pitiful than tasteless; and Faron Carter's tournament citations, his stuffed world's records.

The second showpiece was the air-conditioned station wagon with the electric everything and the power-assisted altogether. It was cream-colored and had tooled Naugahyde upholstery. After ten months, none of it was scuffed; they had no children. I want my Gran Torino scuffed, thought Jeannie. I want the rich simuwood cherry-and-oak body paneling covered with a little one's scratches. I want some li'l peeper to give me fits hacking around with the Selectshift Cruise-O-Matic, the RimBlow Deluxe three-spoke steering wheel or the Power-plus positive windows. I wanna look down at the optional color-keyed vinyl floor carpet and see *bubble gum* with them precious toothprints.

At each of her temples, Jeannie had barely visible veins that showed under her film of skin. You wouldn't want to touch them either. When Jeannie used to poise heels together on the fifty-yard line, the white bulbs of rubber making a pale circle around her flawless twirling, her perfect, silver-sateen-enclosed, indented buttocks sent half the audience into a jack-off frenzy that made them blur out the first quarter of the game itself.

And Jeannie knew that. Twirling, dropping to one knee for the catches, then prancing downfield in a mindlessness now growing culturally impossible, she was a simple pink cake with a slot. And two broad bleacher-loads wanted a piece of it. It was a whole civilization up shit creek in a cement canoe without a dream of a paddle.

Now with veins in her temples ready to leak and a skull to jump out of its pale, thin envelope, she wanted to buy things. And it only made her sorry when she did; not that Carter went after her. He would come home and there would be some unpaid-for showpiece and Jeannie weeping by the TV and drawing flower-print tissues in decorative colors from a gift box. And Carter would feel sorry because he had just come from the Lions Club luncheon where things seemed fine; and here they'd gone from bad to worse.

They had gotten to the point of collection agents; and sometimes when Carter came in from guiding he found Jeannie in terror because some beef-fed muscle-man had been around putting the heat on; or had perhaps gone so far as to garnishee the infrared barbecue oven or intercept some panel truck trying to deliver a love seat.

Years ago, in the lid of a makeup box she still used, she had printed this message from a book by Roger L. Lee called *Baton Twirling Made Easy*:

There is a tendency when strutting to shorten one's stride. If one allows his stride to become less than thirty inches, he will crowd the first rank in the band. This, naturally, will cause the first rank to shorten its stride, throwing the entire band off.

Today, again, Carter had to explain that he couldn't have every customer that came to the dock; there was another guide as much in demand as he was; and a kid who was the real McCoy was having a skiff built.

"Couldn't you talk to Myron," she pleaded.

"Myron doesn't have anything to do with it. He just tells you what's happened after it has happened."

There was no use explaining. When Jeannie first saw Myron Moorhen at his desk with the yellow sheets and the columns of numbers streaming from his finger-tips to the word TOTAL, something imprinted. Myron had the combination; and if you could only talk to him right, the immense empty space would send runners and connections toward one another.

And everything would be O.K.

OLIE SLATT SAID, "I WOULDN'T TRADE THIS certificate for a king's ransom. It cost me an arm and a leg to get to the southernmost U.S. and this right here is your high point."

"I hope she works out that way," said Dance, "but to tell you the truth, I expected to see you a little sooner than this and now I'm booked up sixteen days straight."

"What does that mean?"

"It means the soonest you could fish with me would be seventeen days from today."

"But what about my damn certificate! I up-chugged for ten hours!"

"Wait a darn second now, Mr. Slatt. This certificate

is good for a day's guiding. You can go with the other boy on the dock here, the old boy in fact I learned everything I know off of."

Olie Slatt was wearing a green plaid suit today, a little short at all its cuffs like a Pinky Lee outfit, except that Slatt was rawboned and pared off to a kind of resistant and cartilaginous surface that seemed implicitly violent in this wax-museum suit.

"Where do I find this other one?" Slatt's pale and sullen face seemed to hang from the ring of his mouth.

"Right there in the bait shack."

"I mean, look at me. Do I look like a rich man? Do I look like a man who can pay Howard Johnson sixteen times in a row to go out fishing on the seventeenth? What kind of queer breed of odds and ends do you have to get down here for you to think like that?"

"Well, you go in there and ask for Faron Carter and give him your certificate. That old boy is a regular fish hawk. If it's in Monroe County and swims, he'll put it in the boat."

Olie Slatt turned as he crossed the lawn. The vent of his plaid coat was agape over his shining rump. "I whooped up ten hours of pie filling for that paper," he said. "My nose is still burning and my gut feels like a mule kicked me. So, don't you nor your sidekicks never try to put me off nor hand me down the line because I'll come back lickety-split and be on you like a dog without a mother." By this time Carter was in the bait-shack doorway listening in. "—I mean to hightail it back to Montana ten days from now with a trophy under my arm or I'm going to know the reason why. I have spent my leisure hours on the Missouri after paddlefish and saugers and dreaming of one day coming home to Roundup with a tropical trophy. Everybody knows why I am here. My reputation depends on my comin home with the goods." All the time Dance watched him, Slatt was twisted around on his shining butt so you could see each button of his plaid suit fastened, his hamstrings sprung taut under the thin white socks as he flexed with irritation from head to toe; and Dance, already nonplused by existence in general, looked at Olie Slatt and thought he acted like a frog in a cloud of fruit flies.

SKELTON WAS MAKING AN INCISION IN THE skin of the fuselage over the center of its only real room when the telephone rang.

"Tom, Cart."

"Hey, Cart. What do you need?"

"How's your skiff coming along?"

"Powell's got a coat of paint on the inside. One more and I can hang the engine."

"You want to guide a week from today?"

"Yes."

"I got me a sportsman here from the state of Montana."

"Sign him up, Cart."

"If you can get him a Citation fish, I think he'll mount it; and I'll see you get the kickback from the taxidermist."

Skelton said, "Tell him a week today at eight-thirty."

Skelton worked for some time making an opening in the fuselage where he had inscribed the long oval shape with a grease pencil. In the yard, he had a clear Plexiglas crown that had been a component from a field radar station. As they said in Key West, it had belonged to us'n, meaning U.S.N., and Skelton had laid hands on it for next to nothing. Within a day, he slid the great bubble into position on his opening, bolted it over a hand-cut gasket, and for good measure sealed it with silicone putty.

Now when he entered the fuselage and closed its compression doorway, he could look up to an immense oval of blue sky, almost never without at least one bird. And when the sun went down, it was as though he were in a planetarium.

He had one long table in the room; and the bunk bed was under the bubble. The bed itself was like a normal two-story bunk bed, except that there was no lower bunk; that area was storage multiples and a single shelf for his Zenith Transoceanic radio and the books he was reading—still Bohlke's *Fishes* and D'Arcy Thompson's *On Growth and Form*—trying to be a better guide.

The Zenith was superb for picking up remote country music stations:

> *Someday, when our dream world finds us,*
> *And these hard times are gone . . .*

And the cooking facilities were a salvaged kitchen from a Mobile trawler that went down between Washerwoman and American shoals full of shrimpers too drunk to drown.

Skelton's every effort was toward being a single-member, intentional community. Faced with the impossibility of cloning, it was imaginable that he would mate. But he was still sketching things in. His little piece of land included a cistern; and when he rebuilt the catchment for it (couldn't see yet how to incorporate it with the fuselage), he would start the garden. Then he would begin culling his guide schedule to one day's fishing a week with people he wanted to see. The bulk of the rest of his time would be used in aimless and pointless research in the natural world, from biology to lunar meditation; all on the principle, the absolute principle, that ripeness was all.

COMMUNISM, THOUGHT GOLDSBORO SKELTON— one should really say Commonism, which is the way he thought of the word—has had God knows a baleful and ruinous influence on the world; but the one major Greaser among world Commonists, Fidel (Skelton called him Fido) Castro, had done him an immeasurable favor when he decided to release Bella Knowles's husband, Peewee, from the Isle of Pines, where he had served some doubtless sorry hours atoning for the one manly thing he had ever done: run a boatload of Springfields to a handful of counterrevolutionaries in Camagüey so worn out they turned the little insurance adjuster over to the Fidelistas out of tedium vitae and small hope of recompense; Peewee Knowles had just been trying to pay off his swimming pool, like any other citizen high and dry on the Morris Plan.

What occasioned this outburst of thought in which Skelton actually thanked Fidel Castro for repatriating Bella's husband was a long inquiry on Bella's part about his former wife. After forbearing her cross-examination, Goldsboro Skelton shocked her into final silence.

"She had tits like *that*," he said of his long-gone spouse, "and when she died, I threw a fiver in the hole and closed a chapter in my life. She had Bright's disease, a ten-pound liver, and left a quarter of a million to the D.A.R., on the long shot America would quit producing people like me and our son."

"Your son is a little odd. And your grandson—!"

"They are perfect."

"Goldsboro."

"Perfect."

"Uh-huh."

"And the next time you answer me like that, I'll have you and your musical background up in north Miami making parakeet-training records."

"So long as I'm back in time to see them wheel the ninny down Duval Street Easter time in his mosquito-proof bassinet."

"Why have I let you sass me and answer me back so long?"

The old man thought, We've all got a story, don't we; and it's always a good one. Absolutely always. The thing that excited him in his seventieth year was that it may all have been the same story.

IN THE BEEHIVE TWILIGHT OF ROOSEVELT BOU-levard, seagulls veered around light poles to the murmur of vouching salesmen. And Thomas Skelton strolled the charter-boat docks with an increasing sense that somebody had his number.

In school physics books, "force diagrams" illustrated balls being acted upon by various vectors of force; the question is, if I am the ball, which way do I go? Do I, he thought, for example, go the way of all good things? Do I go for broke? Do I pass go? Do I go man go? Do I say go away? Do I go in my pants? Or do I simply call for my belongings and wait until called upon to stop by higher forces acting upon the simple ball of self. The answer was the simple "Dunno" of the Joe Palooka comic strips. When what we dread the most occurs, a loss of "features," we look around and say, "Me? I dunno."

SKELTON SAT IN HIS QUARTERS. HE WONDERED that you could say the right word in a bad situation and all hell would break loose. He had found the word and said it and all hell had broken loose. Now a military tribunal had found him guilty of obstructing the war effort.

World War II was just going to have to piss up a rope without him. He had perhaps made a little too much of Adolf Hitler and the Miami Press Club; but his present removal was less a consequence of that than it was of his running commentary on the possibilities of glory in war, which, it was said, demoralized the men; especially those types of enlisted men who found themselves at Fort Benning in 1943, a cast-iron year, obliged to jump daily from the practice tower or on the static line from the lumbering planes of the Airborne; who often as not came from one of those almost vanished and newsless backwaters ungoverned by external event or government adventure which had long since turned, blood and bone, to the more reliable products of human communities, season, and acts of God.

These "yokels," as they were known among an officer corps that holed up with cotton-chopping thirteen-year-olds for a giggle, these yokels thought that Skelton was as funny as Skelton's own girlfriend back in Key West thought he was, with her genius intelligence and near-photographic memory; and her curious, not to say outrageous, special history.

But one bird colonel out of Long Island, New York, who "knew from funny" and who would some years later be a charter subscriber to Mortimer J. Adler's series of the Great Books of the Western World, resolved to snare this bird before he pissed away all the morale his phalanx of cannon fodder owned.

Inside of ten days, he had Skelton shut up tight as a drum in the Fort Benning jail and ready to embark upon the duration at hard labor.

And within forty-eight hours of that, the bird colonel and future Great Books subscriber found himself (bused at his own expense) on Peachtree Street in Atlanta in a quiet, freshly abandoned insurance office chatting with a retired senator and one Goldsboro Skelton of Key West, Florida, son of the last important wrecking master on that island, heir to a now lost salvage fortune, and apoplectic, entrepreneurial maniac, crook, and political manipulator. Skelton sat with one of his counterparts, a senator of the old Soufland school, a preposterous amalgamation of the man on the Quaker Oats box and a full-grown marsh weasel.

Now Goldsboro Skelton didn't know anything about Georgia politics, except that they were rotten; but everyone knew that. Goldsboro Skelton didn't know very much about mainland Florida politics either, when you came right down to it; but he could in an hour's phoning form an ineluctable bridge of crooks to any state capitol within two thousand miles. The cybernetics of semi-respectable crime and its system of internal favors is a communal network as handsome in its way as the whorls of the chambered nautilus.

"Senator," said Goldsboro Skelton, "tell our friend the colonel what you just told me."

The senator quickly rose to accustomed orotundities about the "plugged nickel" he wouldn't dream of giving for the colonel's "sorry and worthless ass" if he didn't find a way of putting young Skelton on the island of Key West within twenty-four hours, all papers of clearance in hand to shut him of the U.S. Army and those "piss-faced nincompoops" like the colonel himself who were allowed to torment youngsters in Georgia while grown men were out giving the Axis what for.

"Gentlemen," said the colonel, trying desperately to forget Long Island and find a way into the mechanism of manipulation these highhanders from East Jesus convinced him existed. "You're trying to make a horse's ass of me."

"Colonel," said Skelton, "if you knew how close the ass of a horse was to actual glue and dog food . . ." He fluttered his hand to let the colonel finish his thought.

There was a reconvening in the army, after which Skelton was found gone of brain and sent home to Key West on a mental.

Years later when the retired colonel, now a leg man for Lever Brothers soap, thumbed open the Syntopicon to the Great Books to find something to stir his soldier's memories, some nugget from Thucydides for instance, the words DOG FOOD would come to him and there would live again in his mind, more than his Exploits Against The Enemy, that day on Peachtree Street when being a horse's ass had been the better part of valor. At such a time, he could turn to the wop-and-kike mob that had inundated his Long Island with a cozy, sold-out feeling that readied him for the millennium, senility, alienation, and dyspepsia.

DOCTOR BIENVENIDA HAD DONE THE IMPOSSIBLE. He had escaped from Cuba with his own finely trained person and he had managed to spring his practice too. Forty-six prosperous Havanans flew the coop to Cayo Hueso; so that, professionally, Bienvenida missed hardly a beat, little more than the time it took to make the ninety-mile ride in his own Hatteras sport-fisherman. Consequently there remained in his tone with his patients a lack of salesmanship, a bluntness of a kind that makes patients believe. He had Jeannie Carter before him now, and he leaned forward slowly to deliver his message, so that his stethoscope dangled free of his chest and his blue jowls made an imperceptible swell forward.

"*He died*," said the doctor. Jeannie Carter was so tense that when she stood up from the Naugahyde seat her sweating behind made a tearing sound. She reached around and plucked the seersucker from her thighs.

"*He died?*"

"Afrai' so."

"Oh, but doctor!"

Jeannie began jumping around the doctor's office, both feet together in a pompon dither reminiscent of her fifty-yard-line sprints at Orlando High.

"It's goody-goody gumdrop!" That sort of thing.

The rabbit had passed away (she was not so blunt as the doctor) and a little one would soon be wedging its way into Sardineland ready for the life of hotcakes. Jeannie thought of the stork.

Now, after running down football fields to a thousand erections rising in salute, Jeannie Carter did not really believe the death of the rabbit meant the coming of the stork. But helplessly the big white bird appeared to her on glistening wings; with a rather biggish beak, to be sure. And a kid in a hankie.

When Carter came home that evening, tired, yet cautiously eyeing the living room for anything new, Jeannie kissed him with a robust suggestion of congratulations.

"Hon," she said, "you're okay."

"What do you mean?"

"Looks like you up and hit the bull's-eye. Wasn't zif you lacked the know-how! Ha, ha!"

"You in a family way, Jeannie?"

"Yes sir, honey, I am."

"Seems like a real miracle." Carter himself envisioned the stork as something like Mothra, the flying Jap winged bug of the late-night horror show, *Creature Feature*.

Carter headed into the Florida room. Carter was tired from poling his skiff all over hell's half acre and he sat on the couch in his khaki guide's clothes and put his feet up. Jeannie followed a few moments later, suddenly full of spirit and even, frankly, *joie de vivre*. She had two demonstration flash cards depicting indistinct blobs and discolorations on a white background. Carter thought they were fetuses.

"Now Cart," she said, beginning to stroll up and down, "don't look bored because you was the one earlier this week what asked me to explain the difference between a pyrolytic self-cleaning oven and a catalytic self-cleaning oven."

"I'm paying the fuck attention. Aw, Jesus . . ." he moaned. He was trying to make the connection between his wife and the self-cleaning oven.

"I believe that you are, Cart. I believe that. Now pictured here is a section of an actual oven panel from a General Electric pyrolytic oven that has been soiled with prune-pie spillover." She turned the card over; it was blank on the other side. "The cleaning cycle is completed and no sign of the prune-pie spillover remains!"

She held up another flash card with a similar mess depicted. "Here you have the cheaper catalytic-oven panel soiled with the same prune-pie spillover." Jeannie rotated the card; the reverse was identical to the facing side: a mess. "After a five-hour baking period there is no noticeable removal of the prune-pie spillover. *And even after one hundred and sixty-eight hours at 400 degrees Fahrenheit, most of the prune-pie spillover remains on the catalytic oven panel!*"

With simple cougar-like grace, Cart rose from the couch and began to stalk his wife. A bit of foam gathered at the corner of his mouth.

THE SKIFF WAS FINISHED. SKELTON WENT OVER it, standing back at the bait wells and looking to follow the curve of the cockpit coaming; it faired forward to the casting deck without a dogleg. It was thoroughly finished, with every corner radiused off and smooth. Skelton wrote out the check.

"You won't believe this but a man came in here," said James Powell, "wearing no shoes and old navy pants with a rope to hold them up and kind of a sheet and offered me ten thousand dollars for this boat."

"That was my father."

"He dresses funny."

"He is trying to keep me from guiding."

"You are going to guide then—"

"Course I am!"

"Buy a gun."

"News gets out, doesn't it."

"News like that does."

They wheeled the skiff out by hand on the trailer through the corrugated shed door. Miranda's car, Miranda inside, was parked in the alley. Skelton lifted the tongue of the trailer over the ball of the hitch and clamped it.

"Thank you, James. The skiff turned out a mile prettier than I even hoped."

"I'm pleased myself. Take me for a ride some day."

"I promise."

"I didn't build that for a coffin, you know."

"It's beautiful," said Miranda. She drove, Skelton constantly looking back to see how it was trailing; the bow loomed in the rear window. "Does it mean a lot to you?"

"It will."

"When?"

"When I have paid for it and put some fish in the box and some hours on the engine. Right now it's just beautiful and beautiful isn't very interesting."

"What about Brueghel, Vermeer, and Cézanne."

"They don't build boats."

"You're a redneck."

"I'm worse, I'm a commercial fisherman. I'd pour water on a drowning man."

"What are those numbers for?"

"Registration."

"The orange sticker?"

"Commercial fishing sticker. —No, the boat means plenty; but there is a kind of letdown when you get something you want that bad."

"I wish I knew what your plan was."

"My plan is to go directly to heaven."

"That was my father's plan. He became an Episcopal priest. Until then he was interested in heaven. After that he was mostly concerned with blooded horses. After horses it was a lady who hunted foxes on horses."

"What did that lead to?" The boat trailed easy.

"A blessed event. My mother took an apartment near Canaveral, divorced my father, and married a realtor. The realtor lost his shirt when NASA moved to the Houston Space Center and all those subdivisions went back to frog pond. Then my mother broke her back in a jeep accident during the Audubon Christmas bird-count competition. The realtor left her and now she lives alone with the blessed event, my half brother. My father handed him over so he could go to Florence and live on the Lungarno with the girl who ran the bake sale at the church picnic, a nymphomaniac golf instructor. My father is addicted to ether and their place stinks. She hangs out at American Express and has a room of her own behind the Duomo for her assignations, usually with buyers from stateside gift shops, not necessarily men . . . But my mother is happy, though she misses all the NASA scientists. Many of them were bird watchers."

"And your dad found his heaven with a cross-sexed nympho bake-salesman in the city of Michelangelo."

"Do I turn here?"

"Next block."

"Well, he did find something. When do you plan on finding heaven?"

"I had what you might call a vision. Half a dozen little brainstorms about living right and being free. Now they weren't any of them simple; but I didn't half expect to have a fight over them. It looks like if I am going to hang in there with the rest of the carnivores, I'm going to have to draw some lines. Nothing obvious. Just some curving friendly lines with two-way turnstiles. —Pull up side of the dry shed there."

"Two-way turnstiles."

"On my Jesus Freeway."

"Is this a joke?"

"Stop right here. You have a responsibility as a motorist. I'll back the trailer in the shed. What we need here is Our Lady of the Skiff; though the record seems to indicate that she does not back small craft or in fact anything under fifty feet unless it has a teak deck or exceptional electronics."

He backed the skiff in without event, detached the trailer; and Miranda parked outside the shed. Skelton stayed to watch them hang the big Evinrude engine, bringing it on a chain from the fork lift and swinging it down on the transom. Skelton gazed at the bright new powerhead, anodized and precise under a veil of light oil. The pulse pack was visible between the wedge of finned cylinders. And the electrical harness sent out its leads and cables to various sealed junctures in the powerhead. Skelton stared, the sound of traffic faraway in his ears.

This like his books, fuselage, imaginary garden, family, loves, religion, and private history was an indispensable component of the spiritual survival multiple he was inventing for himself; and through which he intended to sandwich himself between earth, sea, and stars with the fit a waffle has within a waffle iron; or the kind of mortising James Powell had performed in his skiff; less a seamlessness than the kind of laminated strength a scar has.

While the skiff was being set up, Skelton proposed, they would go up to Big Pine and have something to eat at the Baltimore Oyster House. A geriatrical hippie in an MG came *that* close to nailing them head on; then nihilistically waved to them as he shot by, as though on a Final Mission. They cruised through Saddlebunch and Skelton could see the area of mangroves penetrated by the creek in which he had lost contact with the Rudleighs. Just past Saddlebunch, Miranda began an oral outrage that lasted till Sugarloaf Key, Skelton gaping wanly through the windshield. A Greyhound passed in the opposite direction, the driver leaning forward on the wheel in the professional slump. Did he see? The bus's brake lights flashed three times in the rear-view mirror. He did. Skelton's face compressed in a lizard grimace, and misfocus crossed his eyes like a momentary shadow. Wave to Sonny in the Gulf Station; he thinks I'm alone. On Summerland Key, wave to Bud in the Sinclair; he sees I'm with a girl. A little dock bar there on the left, on a raft; friendly place but no pool table. Skiffs moored in its shadow; lobster traps piled all over and ocean both ways; God if they will leave that ocean alone, I can take it all. Osprey goes over; kestrels on the wire watching for mice where they mow the shoulder; and anole lizards, of course, whose translucent rib cages and generally green delicateness recommend themselves to the little falcons. Big Pine and the Baltimore Oyster House.

"Hungry?" Skelton asks.

"I was."

"Oh God, Miranda."

They sat at the bar. The cook and owner was a former submariner, a burly bald man who carried a wordless moral impact Skelton supposed Sam Johnson must have owned.

"What are you going to have?" Miranda asked.

"She-crab soup."

"Me too. Can you split an order of oysters?"

"What kind of oysters?" Skelton asked the barmaid.

"Both," she said.

"Chesapeakes and Apalachicolas," Skelton said to Miranda.

"You say."

"Apalachicolas. It's a state industry. And give us a pitcher."

The oysters arrived shortly. Skelton said, "Let's just eat these off the one plate instead of dividing them up."

Skelton squeezed lime on an oyster, raised its barnacled shell to his lip, and pushed the occupant into his mouth. Word had it Apalachicola was having water problems; better enjoy these while you can. What an idea. My people have been eating Apalachicola oysters for a hundred years; I object on the basis of family. Spiders have so much bug-killer in them they can't make symmetrical webs either. Skelton looked over at Miranda to reiterate his conviction of general pointlessness; but he noticed a button on her shirt pulled taut between her breasts, tilted almost enough to slip through the buttonhole; he knew those appendages to be slightly larger and slightly firmer than well-made Cuban flan and that concrete thought about something desired made him lose interest in despair. He had long since learned that the general view was tragic; but he had simultaneously learned that the trick was to become interested in something else. Look askance and it all shines on. The hope of reward in this line of religion was to be able to gaze with boredom straight into the big black hole, pausing only to wipe the face of your pocket watch with a clean linen handkerchief so that its next owner can trade it in on a new Bulova along with the gold he has knocked out of your indifferent teeth. After all, who on earth slipping it to a truly desired woman can seriously interest himself in the notion that the race is doomed; at such a time, the very thought is a flourish. Afterward, in the little death, a universal view spreads its arms; and the received world has "features" looped and looped in Nietzschean returns.

Skelton for his part, though blessed with good health and the lack of ordinary worries, was thankful that it had been since the trick Dance, Carter, and the Rudleighs had played him that he felt that separation of himself from the people and objects amid which he lived.

Two nights earlier he had gotten so frightened that Dance would kill him that he had cried; but he never felt the yawning that came between himself and everything when his essential facilities for control began to lock up.

Studying biology—at the end—he lost the connection between the sessile polyp he was dissecting and the firmament, in effect the kingdom-and-glory; or that at least was his first sign; within two hours, only Thorazine drove Satan from his eyes long enough for him to reform the connections between himself and what was palpably not himself. One more week and he was in Key West again, where it was widely reported that he had "lowered his expectations." He wants to be a guide, people said, looking at each other with signification, out in a damn boat all the doo-dah day.

Skelton looked aside to Miranda. Is this a loose woman? When he was young, he was always falling in love; once with a floozy from the base named Joyce; he had a souped-up Chevy BelAir then with a three-quarter-race engine, scavenger headers, and so on; and he and Joyce would take a bottle and go up the keys where Joyce would sometimes run along the four-inch bridge railings and—twice—fall off, missing the abutments, somehow. Joyce was loose as a goose. She chipped in with him on a set of slicks so they could drag-race sailors on A1A. A friend of Skelton's told him that if Joyce had as many dicks sticking out of her as she'd had sticking in her she would look like a porcupine. Skelton punched him dutifully; they drifted apart and Skelton kept the racing slicks.

"Know what?"

"What."

"Still haven't seen my old man. Hasn't showed up since he was around your place. But I want to ask you something. Do you think he was serious when he was asking you for a date?"

"No. He was making fun."

"Well, he's not an unkind person."

"Can you eat that last oyster?"

"No, you."

"I will. Well, what kind of father is he?"

"The best. And I been reviewing his performance since I was real little. He is always checking to see how things add up. He taught me how to step to one side about everything I looked at, always change the angle."

"Does that make for a happy life?"

"Probably not. So what."

"Is this upsetting you?"

"A little."

"What has he done?"

"He got thrown out of the army during World War II and came home and invented a new kind of infrared film for night photography and got decorated. The army paid him a percentage on the film and he used the money to open a whorehouse, a blimp factory, and a reading room for Catholic-anarchist literature. He closed the reading room when he learned anarchists had fought with the White Russians. Then he opened it again when he learned the Communists had suppressed Basque anarchists in the Spanish Civil War. He is an idealist. —He kept a horse."

"In Key West?"

"An American Saddlebred with rubber shoes. He could swim it to Christmas Island and gallop in the sea-shells."

Miranda drove back. She was an aggressive driver and a tailgater; and when she passed she stayed too long in the left lane. Skelton hated riding with her. When they got to the dry shed, he told her to meet him at the dock.

The skiff was ready; they put the fork lift under the hull and backed out of the shed with it and lowered it into the water. Skelton got in and walked it around to the gas dock, where he fueled up. The engine started readily and he let it idle for a moment. Then he pushed off and backed around far enough that he could turn and pull out alongside the sponging skiffs, the old Johnson rum-running boat, and crawfish boats moored along the sea wall. When he had clearance, he put it up on a plane, hearing the strange two-stroke exhaust rap of the engine. The fully powered boat seemed to have a kind of loft and control that he had hoped for. He swung under the Eisenhower Causeway and could feel the flat-bottom hull skidding as he knew it would; but the chines didn't catch, so the rate of slide was predictable. He powered it through the turn near Bachelor Officers' Quarters, past the gaudy Cuban commercial boats that looked like dismasted sailboats, then out through the gap at Sigsby for a five-minute shakedown. He ran it past the little key there in a foot of water at 4,000 rpm and abruptly shut it down. The boat settled levelly without dropping the stern and fouling the prop on the bottom. He ran it up on a plane, snaking it off a little to put the prop away from the bottom a few inches, and headed for the dock at 2,900, its slowest planing speed, with a sense of complete satisfaction.

In three minutes, he rounded the island to Chambers Street where he could see, a hundred yards before he shut down, Miranda sitting on one of the guides' lockers at the dock, talking to Jeannie Carter and Nichol Dance.

Wild horses belonged to that category of things that could not have made Skelton bring these three together on purpose, nor any collaboration of all the tea in China and months of Sundays. On days of more than twenty-knot wind, the foam lines began to build on the ocean and any bird that so much as raised its wings got the kind of scudding trip before superior force that Skelton felt himself now getting, as these clusters formed and foolish lives like his father's began to break up. Something was afoot.

Nichol Dance fended the boat and threw two half-hitches around the bow cleat; Skelton reversed his engine against the line and swung the stern in alongside the dock and shut down.

"What's up?"

"Your girl here wants to know why I'm going to shoot you if you guide."

Jeannie released the long trilling laugh that had, after the baton, become, in effect, her trademark. It was her song; and she used it to skewer a few half-formed thoughts like shish kebab. Skelton climbed up on the dock.

"What are you laughing at?"

"The thought that Nichol could hurt a . . . a fly!"

When she knew as well as anybody that the personable Hoosier had blown that exercise boy to Kingdom Come; and in a moment of pique neatly gaffed Roy Soleil for ridiculing him. But hurt a fly!?

That is why Miranda said, "Come off it," with that particular woman-to-woman force that scares men. Skelton sat on the wooden locker with the others.

"Why in the worl' do you want to guide anyway?" Jeannie asked Skelton himself.

"It's been sort of a process of elimination," said Skelton.

"Well, you oughta had seen my husband about the time when he come in with his skin burnt half off!"

Dance was looking a little foolish; he didn't see how he could reiterate his threat or add some credence to it without reminding everybody of TV.

"That's a pretty little skiff though," Jeannie observed. "I bet you're real proud of it."

"I am."

"Best skiff I seen yet," Dance said.

"And I know it'll mortally fly," Jeannie said, "with that one-twenty-five Starflite Evinrude settin on that transom waitin to flat shut down these other turkeys."

"Aw well, who knows . . ." Skelton could do without Jeannie's ascription of mechanical superiority here just now. But Dance didn't take it that way; he smiled and listened, always a man who knew who he was. He talked without studying your eyes to see what you thought of what he said.

"But I sure will say this. Cart has never lost a day's wages with his Merc. That old Thunderbolt ignition and Power-Trim just seem to be the combination for a workin fool like Cart."

Skelton could hardly pay attention; he was in his trance. There was Nichol the same way. The Eternal Revenue Service is in the wings. But the girls with their race's gift for the here and now were casting sidelong glances at one another. Jeannie's skewer laugh shot forth again and she said, "What Key West needs with a beginner guide beats me for starters!"

"Your ass is sucking swamp water," said Miranda.

"I guess that's about as lady-like as I'd expect from a Mallory Square weirdo all right."

"What clodhoppers expect in the way of lady-like doesn't interest me that much."

"Doesn't interest . . . ! How would a poke in your fancy snoot do, schoolmarm?"

Miranda, *mirabile dictu*, sucker-punched poor Jeannie, fist to jaw with the sound of flounder on butcher's marble. But Jeannie came back kicking and clawing and making a long intermittent whine of rage. There was only a long flailing moment of this, ending with terrific yanks on each other's hair, which was long enough that they could stand a yard and a half apart ripping and hauling. Dance got Miranda and Skelton got Jeannie and took them away from each other. They were crying.

Jeannie ran across the street to the Sandpiper, and Miranda went inside the bait shack to doctor herself.

Dance shook his head. "I didn't know whether to shit or go blind. I believe they'd hurt each other."

Myron Moorhen came to the door.

"What happened?"

"Nothing, Myron. Go count."

"You wouldn't shoot a sweet guy like me," Skelton said.

"I wouldn't want to."

"But can't you tell I'm going to work now that I have the boat?"

"I'm not thinking that far ahead."

"But just figuring I do—"

"Then you'll spend the rest of your life dead; and I'll spend mine in the joint. You'd have possibly the better shot at eternal reward."

"But you might bail it out with last-minute repentance."

"I ain't a Catholic."

Miranda came out of the bait shack. "Honey, let's go home." Dance walked with them to the parking lot.

"Night now," Dance said and walked across to the Sandpiper, where he matched the bartender for the jukebox, won, and played *The Easy Part's Over* by Charley Pride; plus two old Waylon Jennings hits.

"Where's Jeannie at?"

"She's around here some place. She's been here three nights tryin her damndest to throw Myron some tail; but he runs like a rabbit."

Jeannie, to be precise, was in the ladies', dabbing at her wounds and taking some easy maneuvers with the baton, around the waist, figure eight between the legs, little toss behind the back, drop to one knee: Dah-*DAH!*

She had her custom baton: thirty inches long, eleven-sixteenths of an inch in diameter and seventeen ounces in weight—just as big as it could be without dragging at her routine. Here in the ladies' she ran through all nine rudiments as a warm-up (*Wrist Twirl, Figure Eight, Cartwheel, Two-Hand Spin, Pass Around the Back, Four-Finger Twirl, Beating Time, Aerial Work, and Salute*); then she put the baton down and climbed up on the toilet so she could see out through the chicken-wire window to the bait shack across the way.

MIRANDA SAID SHE COULDN'T HELP IT. SKELTON sighed.

"Honestly, I couldn't watch that little chippy take on that way without calling her."

"Miranda, a cat fight is a terrible thing to see. Can we not talk about it?"

"All right. Am I badly scratched?"

"Sort of."

"My scalp hurts. That whore gave me some yanks."

"I'll bet. It looked like you had both gone ape-shit."

"Really?" She grinned and turned down White Street in time to see Skelton's father streak into the alley past the Gulfstream Market. At the end of the alley, Miranda stopped the car and Skelton caught a flicker of motion behind three galvanized garbage pails. "Keep it up!" Skelton called. "*You're on your way!*"

MYRON LOOKED UP AT THE CLOSING OF THE bait-shack door. Say it isn't so. Humming a samba,

Jeannie was twirling her baton and shedding her clothes. Myron Moorhen made frantic mute signs with his hands. He wants my pear-like tits, she thought, spinning spinning spinning. She advanced upon Myron's agape face, once more a joyous pink cake with a slot behind the glittering baton, Myron waving frantic in the rising ardor of her wordless samba.

Jeannie said breathlessly, "A youngster building up her wrist and forearm twirling a seventeen-ounce baton will have in later years terrific power for certain activities!" Jeannie's speech was punctuated by the flushing of a toilet and the stepping of her husband, a member of fraternal organizations as well as of the republic, from the bathroom.

Cart was awful surprised. What Jeannie was doing here in the bait shack was worse than real different.

CARTER TOOK JEANNIE WEEPING TO THEIR showpiece home in the gelid air of the station wagon. He turned on the religious station to build a background. There was a small chat about the coming of Christ in your democratic manner: "Joseph and Mary really clicked. There is no two ways about it. *But . . .* when they found out their kid was God, *frankly*, it threw them for a loop."

Carter pulled up in the driveway and took the baton from Jeannie's hands. She began to weep. "Please Cart please please please."

"Every time you get this sonofabitch out of storage, Jeannie, we run into a problem."

"Please Cart please."

"I come into the bait shack where I make my bread and butter and find you been dukin out some schoolteacher and five minutes later you're doin your baton routine in the altogether with vodka on your breath for my accountant! And tellin him it builds up a girl's fore-arm for jackin guys off!"

"Oh but Cart!"

"You're sick Jeannie and your baton is sick."

He began to form a loop with the baton between his great guide's hands as Jeannie's wail rose to something as purely musical as her mad trilling laugh, as deso-late as some final and inconceivable Orlando "never-more." Cart flung the pretzeled baton into the garbage pail, simultaneously discharging a yowling cat from within. Then the two entered their showpiece and stood on the terrazzo, each weeping for his own spavined dream.

WHEN CART REENTERED THE BAIT SHACK My-ron Moorhen recoiled against the trophy wall as though he had been hit by a howitzer.

"Honest, I didn't lay a finger on her!"

A stuffed jack crevalle bounced off Myron's head to the floor. Myron clapped a terrified hand to the spot as though it had been Carter's first blow. Cart was look-ing at the floor patiently; when he raised his head, My-ron shot fifteen feet to the left.

"Honest! *Honest honest honest!*"

"Myron..."

Moorhen shot to the freezer and groped frantically within. He withdrew a frozen kingfish of perhaps twelve pounds. A member of the mackerel family, and therefore long and pointed, a frozen kingfish makes a formidable weapon. Myron raised the frosted blue shape over his shoulder in the "ready" stance Ted Wil-liams has long advocated for batters. His eyes narrowed to a new confidence and his lips opened flat in a vague smile that showed a sharp white line of teeth.

"Myron, relax! You are among friends and this is no clambake."

"What are you going to do to me?"

"Absolutely nothing. Put down that king."

"Not so fast. Tell me what's going to happen to me."

"I already told you nothing is going to happen. Where did that fish come from?"

"Lou O'Connor got it at American Shoals."

"Deep jigging?"

"No, drifting with ballyhoo. He got six altogether."

"Huh. Maybe the run's started."

"Excuse me, Cart, but what uh what was it you were going to do to me?"

"About Jeannie?"

"I think so," said Myron, unobtrusively returning the frozen kingfish to the freezer.

"Well, I was going to tell you that she is just kind of sick right now poor li'l thing and I want *you Myron* to try and forgive her for what *she* done to *you* this evening here."

"Aw Cart, Cart, Cart. Of *course* I forgive her."

"And she said she mm left some underthings . . . ?"

Myron, moving now with reckless freedom, took a wad of nylon and silk from the top drawer of his desk and tossed it, just between a couple of fellows, to Cart.

"Cart, she is awful good with that baton!"

Carter smiled shyly. "You know, Myron, she *ain't* half bad . . . Only, Myron?"

"Whussat, Cart?"

"She don't own her no baton no more."

"Uh, where's it at, Cart?"

"It's one giant step up her ass, Myron."

Myron giggled, "You don't mean that!"

"Oh but I do." Carter had a certain affection for this

lie. "I suppose it'll show up again one of these days," he added.

Guffaws.

SKELTON THOUGHT THAT WHEN WHAT YOU ought to do had become less than a kind of absentee ballot you were always in danger of lending yourself to the deadly farce that surrounds us. The subtlest kind of maladjustment and you plummeted through the tissue surface of the socially lubricated and solvent to that curious helter-skelter of selves which produced such occasional private legislators as Nichol Dance.

Ideas like that, thought Skelton, could set a man to barking. Even a brief soulful howl beside the garbage would help. Even the notions of what wild horses couldn't get you to do acquired an unabstract vigor—to the extent that you could nearly see their luminous manes and screaming nocturnal shapes. Half the time when lives streamed past on parallel courses, a false security developed: and the victim began to imagine that these lifelines did not congest or break down. Too late, the head-ons became apparent and you looked up to scream: The sonofabitch is in my lane! Histories are fused as metal by heat.

There was a knocking on the door of the fuselage. Skelton opened it; it was the wino drill sergeant from next door. "Come in."

"Thank you, sir. Do you have a dog?"

"No, I don't."

"I thought I heard barking."

"I was clearing my throat."

"I was wondering, sir, if you could accompany me to headquarters."

"Next door?" Skelton asked.

"Yes, sir."

"Why?"

"No questions, please."

"All right," Skelton said, thinking, I will lend myself to another's trip as my own leads only to the sillier kind of despair, plus, of course, Hamletism; not to mention mooning and the unenunciated snivel.

Skelton followed the sergeant with civilian dignity. At the door to the hotel, they were saluted by two winos who permitted them to enter the vomit-scented front hall. They ascended the stairway, whose walls approached within inches of Skelton's shoulders. There was a man on duty at the top of the stairs and two men, rather less on duty, out cold in the upper hallway in their own puke, their blurred, raspy faces and crew-cuts communicating precisely what is communicated by a wrecking yard.

Skelton was shown into a room; the door was closed behind him as the light was turned on. The room only had space for a single bed, and Skelton's father was in it looking less mortal than ephemeral; and considerably more dead than alive. He had his fiddle with him.

It was plain that the sheet beneath which his father lay was the one he had worn these last days around town. It had motor oil and dirt all over it, and on the section that covered his feet was a tire print.

"Well," said his father, "I have to make a piece of wreckage of myself so we can have a bedside scene together."

"What are you talking about."

"This." An inclusive gesture.

Skelton refused to reply.

"All right."

"We've all been chasing you. Mother is finally finished with this stuff too I can tell you."

"I wanted to advise you. That is what fathers do."

"Why didn't you just come over to my place. I have been looking for you every which way."

"I didn't have the advice ready. I had to go through a certain number of operational maneuvers, as they say here at headquarters, to get myself down to the level at which I knew what you were going through."

Skelton looked into his palms for a sign.

"I'm not going through anything in particular," Skelton lied.

"Do you think your friend is joking?"

"No. We have just laid out some terrains and a process of natural selection is going on."

"Oh, come on. I thought we'd been over that Darwin baloney. I don't even like it as a figure of speech."

It appeared for a moment that he would actually be sick to his stomach. Skelton could not quite fathom the total degeneration he saw before him. His father's face, often compared to Manolete's, was covered with an uneven stubble; and his hair, always cut short as that of a monk, seemed like a barber-college special. The fingers of his inordinately long and ghostly hands arose to make a point, then faded with its vanishment from his mind. Whether from hunger or obsession, his face had receded from his eyes, isolating them in their sockets with an unmistakable suggestion of madness. Skelton felt a certain embarrassment at his own short-fingered, tough hands in his lap, rough-palmed from the pushpole: another sign that he had come from nowhere; a suggestion he was determined to put the lie to.

"I've had an adventure, I guess," said his father wanly. "Like falling through space. I did some drinking and ended up here. I must think of when I left the army . . . I somehow consumed seven months getting to Key West. The things that happened to me were so foreign to what it seems *could* have happened to me. Much more disturbing than amnesia. You try to date your life around the things that happen to you that you can't understand. When you understand something, it is no longer any good to you. It's neutralized. When I got into the 'bassinet' there for seven months, I was trying to create one of those situations, artificially; and I failed because it was just eccentric. There was no mystery, no real enigma."

"Except to others."

One of his father's eyelids was considerably lower than the other; and when he thought intensively, he usually pushed it up with his forefinger; he did now.

"It even lacked mystery for others. The odd and the mysterious are not the same."

"Okay."

"Then quite naturally I began to try to see what could be done about what was happening to you. I tried a few simple things like offering to buy the boat but my heart wasn't in it. And I knew it ran counter to what you would accept. You have always been dedicated to ordeals as a way of driving your spirit to the place where its first confusions are. I think you've gotten away from that now and I showed you a lot about sidestepping that may have been useful."

"Better than that."

"So anyway—and this will seem a little simple-minded—I had the plan that I would try to condition myself to the point that life could depart almost as a relinquishment, a little release of the will and it would seep away . . . or something, right?"

"Yes, right," Skelton said very nearly inaudibly.

His father laughed. "Everything happened. I got drunk, worked over, run in by the police, thrown out of restaurants. I told these boys here that I was discharged dishonorably from the army and they locked me in the 'brig,' which is the mop closet on the first floor. I know, *funny;* but I was in there two days without anything to eat. I have only been released five hours now."

Skelton in pain glanced to the window where bright palm leaves shuddered in incongruous evening sunlight. And hearing traffic, he thought, How dare anyone go on about his business.

"But I began to find what could not be explained." He drew out his upper plate; it was broken and taped back together. "I got drunk and fell down over in back of Carlos's market and this preacher took my plate out and stepped on it."

"Why didn't you go home!"

"Oh come on." His father's detachment was serene. If there was anything that identified him by blood in place of the dissimilarity of hands, it was this proclivity for slipping the moorings. Skelton's own "ordeals," as his father termed them, his attempt to be sane, *a biologist*, when his actual instincts were less linear, less useful, only led to a bout of hallucinations, featuring drowning, falling, wild horses, endless crowds of driverless automobiles under evidently perfect control hurtling over rough landscapes; and even before Dance had spoken of Charlie Starkweather in the city jail, electrocution, which came to him as a kind of tickling to death, a trampling under electrical horses.

"My first instinct was that this face-off with what's-his-name was a matter of honor."

"Oh God!"

"Well, you'll admit that was the obvious choice."

"I don't admit that!"

"Well you goddamn prima donna! What was the obvious choice then!"

Skelton racked his brains. His father was right. But he didn't have a thing to tell him.

"That's the best I can do," he said, not quite coming clean.

"All right then listen you dumb bunny. Now you can get killed at this thing you're up to. So, you see it through so you know what it is when it comes. Otherwise you are a bystander and nothing could be more disgusting."

They stopped talking. Skelton remembered in his childhood his father explaining to him that he lived in a civilization that was founded from its family life to its government on the principle that the wheel that squeaks the loudest gets the grease.

"Your grandfather," he said now, "is a great American in the way he has learned to work the gaps of control that exist between all the little selfish combines. That is why he has been able to rook the country out of millions without ever getting petty about it. —Now, at my best I have been a transitional figure in trying to get you some idea of his energy and coordinational power— with the conviction that I would be consumed in the process—so that you could use it toward something a little more durable than the kind of power your grandfather has craved so . . . horribly."

He took up his fiddle and all that scarifying instinct for spirals upon spirals of cognition fell from his tormented face; and a turbulent gaze into emptiness that had become less Skelton's birthright than a kind of visitation fell across it. For Skelton's father always felt himself to be poised on the edge of some yawning fissure. One of the ways he crossed it, besides the sports page and its illusion of a constant skein of clear athletic effort in which no one was swept away in time, one of the ways he crossed that fissure was with his fiddle. His head inclined upon it now as though he would fall serenely asleep; the eccentrically long bow indented itself gently against the strings and paused before the opening strains in deepest space. And then the crazy man began *Jerusalem Ridge* pure and howling in a final elevation to the light that Skelton could understand.

SKELTON THOUGHT ABOUT THE ELECTRICAL drill and how it could take the hole of the light socket and modify it to another; hole power; perhaps ridiculous but close to his father and his mysteries. He thought of the vultures you could see circling a pit (usually filled with garbage but never mind that); or how during the eclipse of the sun in 1970, running to the Snipe Keys, he had stopped the skiff when the light started to go out, looked up as proscribed by radio news broadcasts to see half a thousand seabirds circling a black hole in the sky. It was the kind of hole people could create, throwing each other into shadow. But there was something there to be considered, the radios everywhere telling you not to look, the vultures over the garbage pit, the news broadcasts of 1970 reflecting another eclipse and a quarter of a billion people staring into the black hole in the sky. And in his own fractional quadrant of world, Skelton looking to the whirling seabirds and their black pivot and then across the still, mercurial sea darkening as though oxydized by this lunar tropism. The power of nothing.

HIS FATHER WAS LAUGHING, HALF TO HIMSELF. "Four nights ago, I got particularly drunk with these fellows that work the boats, then bum their way up to the Carolinas in the summer. I left them about midnight

I suppose and was crawling, literally crawling, along Eaton Street when a car pulled up and Bella got out. She took about fifty pictures of me creeping down Eaton in my sheet, saying, "Bahyewtiful, bahyewtiful!" the whole while. I suppose she's fanning them out for the old man right now. That won't take him in! He's seen it all ... By the way, he knows your plan and completely disagrees with my interfering."

Skelton thought, That does not surprise; any more than that his father, who had eschewed authority in himself as well as others throughout most of a lifetime, should suddenly attempt to advise and force, however halfheartedly; while his mother, who cultivated durability as another might table manners, was beginning to discover an exasperation with all three men, as anyone would with cheap or highly tuned machinery that constantly needed repairs.

"Well, I don't know what I wanted to tell you. I'm so down now it seems like I could tell you more about what might await you. Even my veins feel slack. And I've only gotten to that place where everything is ironic in a simpleton's way; you know, looking down at people living beyond their means, ridiculing bad taste and so on. That's not very interesting. So I haven't got much to tell you. Except that I wish you'd give up this idea."

"What would you do in my place?"

"I'd go through with it."

"That neutralizes your advice."

"No it doesn't. I have a perspective that I couldn't have if it was me acting."

"Like what kind of perspective."

"A Christian one."

"Why couldn't I have that myself?"

"Because the Christian perspective is one that only

obtains in the third person; otherwise it vanishes in egotism and you become a figure from which ridicule can derive as from Christ himself."

"Well, let me say first of all that I don't believe that for a minute. And then let me remark that when a man goes to such trouble to set up a crisis, I have a certain duty that comes of my respect for him to let that crisis take place."

"I'd say, on the basis of that, that you were a smart little fuck. But I think you're just reacting by temperament and out of your nose for trouble."

"Anyway, it never got me anywhere except a trip to the ward until I started acting on my own instincts and following through. Now what I'm doing and what Nichol is doing are two cases of just exactly that."

"Are you quite sure?"

"No, I'm really not."

Skelton was getting tired of this; and he could see his father was too. So he asked his father to get up and come to his place; and surprisingly he bounded out of bed, the fiddle familiarly in one hand like a tennis racket.

They entered the fuselage, the first time for his father; he beamed around its interior and began dressing as Skelton handed him articles of clothing.

Skelton quite suddenly recalled Nichol Dance. Let's think about this thing head on now. It has become clear that I am liable to forfeit, as they say, my, you know, *life*. What you get in that case is . . . death. Now: what can I expect in the way of a tremendous death? Not much. There are no tremendous deaths any more. The pope, the president, the commissar all come to it like cigarette butts dropped to the sidewalk from the fingers of a pedestrian hurrying on toward some cloudy appointment.

"You got anything to drink?"

"Maybe a beer," said Skelton.

"I disburden myself of a life's discoveries and you offer me a beer."

"What do you want a drink for?"

"I want to get illuminated."

"Well, then you just hold on there—" Skelton took a film canister out of one of his ammunition cases and opened it.

"Lick your finger and stick it in there—"

"Like that?"

"Now lick it off."

"What is it? Is it dope?"

"No. Just do it." He made his father do that three times, then did the same himself.

"All right," said his father, "I trusted you. Now you tell me what that is."

"Mushrooms carefully gathered by South American Indian witch-doctor curandero genius-maniacs."

"Then you gave me dope."

"No, sir. It's another thing."

"I'm a dope fiend," said his father.

"No," said Skelton, "I can tell you about that because I was one of those—"

"How bad was it? I thought that was what you were up to."

"Pretty bad."

"But like what?"

"A little like real flu combined with bad nerves and extreme old age."

"Sounds attractive. Now what I'd like to know is why, on the basis of that, and with my proffered trust, you would pour drugs down my gullet."

"It's not the same thing."

ELAPSE. A ZONE ENSUES: TIME IN CLARITY.

Skelton explained how he had put his shelter together; and said he had wanted a kind of second-floor
compartment but couldn't see how to do it. His father
sat down and started sketching a kind of blister for the
fuselage with a floor suspended on cables; it was made of
tetrahedral sections, some windows, some hinged-on
marine hardware so that it could be vented, the whole
capable of flexion: the sides to fair into the fuselage itself and the floor on its braided cables to be a live surface
("So that each step you take provides part of the next
step"), all drawn in an elegant dry-point style reminiscent of old artist-engineers. His father looked down at
his work and laughed. "Later, we'll talk about how to
keep the rain out."

Skelton walked around in a long silvery orbit, his
hands behind him and his fingers trailing. Starlight came
in overhead like the fine pinpoints of charged water.

"God!" said his father, "can you smell all that top-
soil out there! No wonder the gardens do so well. Jesus,
I can smell all that wet moss under your mother's philo-
dendrons!" He pulled open a drawer beneath the salvaged marine cookstove and burst into laughter. Skelton walked over and looked in: there was some
silverware and a corkscrew. It was pretty funny all
right.

Skelton's father crawled around on the floor, tears
of helpless laughter dripping before him. Skelton took
one last look into the drawer—silverware and corkscrew
maniacally arrayed there—and leaned up against the wall
laughing convulsively.

When his father stood up, Skelton looked at him
dressed in one thing or another from his own sorry

wardrobe; and smiled. "You do look dapper."

"Look what?"

"Dapper."

"*Dapper!*"

"Oh, Lord!"

"Let's have another look in that silverware drawer," his father said. It was the same in there: some knives, forks, spoons; and that corkscrew. Neither of them could take it.

In the eyes of Skelton's father, the effacement of his accumulated sorrows had given way to a silly serenity. And Skelton himself, who had been feeling so narrowly treated by his existence, was on the margin of that horse-laugh magnanimity that reveals new things under heaven every time.

"Let's head for the old plant."

"I'm for it."

The two men hurried through the lunar palm shadows to the warehouse on upper Petronia. They passed a ghostly street sweeper with his own key to the cemetery, and a taxicab with golden interior light bustling down Flagler without a passenger through blue islands of moon shadow.

At the warehouse, Skelton's father lifted a piece of cracked concrete for the key, unlocked the padlock on the corrugated door, and led Skelton inside. "If we play our cards right," said his father, "we are headed for an emotional El Dorado in here, a real jackpot."

Skelton passed him entering and saw vainglory in his father's face. The data base here was decades of folly, the end-all praxis of quixotry.

Inside, the vast rubberoid wreckage of the Southernmost Blimp Works, presided over by a surplus, helium-filled barrage balloon on a swaying cable. Skelton's father hauled in a few feet of cable and released it; the barrage balloon throbbed back into its position up under the ceiling; there was a black flag on its side and the phrase,

MAKE IT MUTUAL.

Skelton found a cylinder full of helium. The two of them filled their lungs with it and began to speak in the voices of Walt Disney ducks.

Skelton said: "In the deep discovery of the subterranean world, a shallow part would satisfy some inquirers; who, if two or three yards were open about the surface, would not care to rake the bowels of Potosí."

His father replied, like a duck too: "The dense and driven Passion, and frightful sweat . . . what none would have known of it, only the heart, being hard at bay—," sighed hugely with a hint of duck noise, picked up a sheet of thick, treated rubber, and quacked, "Oh this too, too solid flesh!"

Skelton's father was looking his inwardly lit best and wore his Manolete face with his witty hooded eyes— possibly now beclouded with those hallucinations that guided earlier Americans; it was the face of his power vision. His other face, his Sinclair Lewis face full-toothed and mildly simian, suggested problems of complexion in his youth and lack of solid moral reference (or blood sugar).

The two men quacked sharply at each other until the helium passed.

"Now son, I want to get back into this advice thing . . . if uh if these walls and floors would stop whipping around I'M A DOPE FIEND and so if you'd uh pay strict mm attention here—" Skelton *fils* was trying his best not to visualize a grave rat combat in the shadows.

"Let's sit down for advice." He patted the air as if to materialize a chair.

The two men sat on rubber sheets that covered most of the floor of the balloonery. The barrage blimp was poised upon its cable with such stillness as to suggest that the cable supported it. Over the doorway, Skelton's now adjusted eyes perceived a portrait of Count Zeppelin with the date of his death, March 8, 1917. Beside the goner hydrogen visionary, a great rigid airship emblazoned *Hansa* rested on a pale, limitless glare of ice.

"Now generally I am told that I am a fine one to talk; so let me offer that as a means of ignoring me. When I suggest something to you, however heartfelt, you remind yourself of my absurd ventures in the manufacturing of blimps, my mental discharge from the army, my unsuccessful family life, and so on. In other words, review my credentials, ha ha! And forget everything I tell you! But *don't* forget, even my whorehouse was a flop! My whorehouse was a flophouse! The floozies turned on me like a hundred raging toucans! They fired upon me with my own Seltzer! In twelve months of operation they never awarded me a freebie! I had a Congolese lesbian who used my Havana Churchills for dildos, then jammed the toilet with them! They peed on my fiddle, overcharged my friends, and gave your grandfather a bigger-than-life dose of Montezuman syphilis with chancres that ran up his body like mink tracks! When I saw what they could do, I gave my life some long thought. First I closed down the anarchist reading room. Then I closed down the Puta Palazzo, as I called my little business. Then I spent five years reading the religious literature of the world, homing in like an atomic pigeon on the Rig-Veda, the Bible, the journal of Pascal, Dostoevsky's *Insulted and Injured* and the *Exemplary Novels* of Cervantes in both the original spic and in the incomparable translation of James Mabbe/Don Diego Puede Ser, ha ha!—the Elizabethan courtier and monster whoremonger of Castille or Cast Steel as the other peerless Diego has it. Well, where was I? Oh, yes. End of religious training. The forging of a bright metal too ductile to be forged! Trainee takes to his bed where he is instructively badgered by his wife and father. The world is viewed through mosquito netting. Lizards and Norway rats are perceived in the moonlight while Cayo Hueso is beddie-bye. A slow but inescapable loathing of his own father begins to form so contrary to subject's wishes he realizes that it is his race's conscience, his utterly bastardized and serenely mongrel and multisexual transnational squid of a people, the cuttlefish of earth, speaking through him when, quite against his wishes, he looks out through the gauze at his own flesh and blood from whose loins needless to say he has leapt in his full deformity, and thinks: *God help me.* Now man in question is an ineffectualist and will not act upon his race's call. But the call is there. This great and powerful animal, your grandfather, this conniving millionaire son of wrecking masters and arch-abrogator of justice is slowly spinning to earth parachuting into his own history with his whores and washed-up coloratura singers, stalked by vague, pusillanimous insurance adjusters in gabardine and color-coordinated, fun-in-the-sun playsuits, and will finally either expire of his own disgust or will be run to ground by men who would ask for the opponent's track record before undertaking to take on a piss-ant! The successor often seems flyblown and rank to the succeeded. Uh, except to me. You have always been liable to revert to your grandfather."

"That's painful for me to recognize. I don't mean that without respect either. But the load is heavy." It was conceivable to Skelton that his earliest compulsive wishes were toward extracting his attention from the fields of changes which he like everyone else had inherited; at one point, phototropic plankton seemed the appropriate antiworld, a collective behemoth only estimable by electronic scanner, formulae, surmises; but even in that, there was a threshold and one which he couldn't penetrate. He suspected lack of intelligence or ability to reason. So on one trip with his most admired professor to study the Loop Current in the Gulf of Mexico, he heard the following between two deckhands:

"Do you believe our Lord will save you?"

"Fuckin A."

This preposterous ontological skirmish had the effect of producing in Skelton the perfect, lingering laugh; one quite embedded now and one which crinkled his face from time to time in giddy spiritual desire. For *something*. For a more penetrating laugh, a victim who said *Bingo-Bango* on the Hill of Skulls and who returned better dividends than War Bonds and compulsory trips to Nepal for the messages you were not getting at home. Even a victim who never was.

"Now," said his father, "one other thing. I ran into my old friend Captain James Davis, formerly skipper of the trawler *Marquesa* and currently doing time as salad chef at Howard Johnson's. What he tells me is that you are always talking to him about me—"

"That's right."

"—and that you always wind up asking him about your mother."

"That's right and he never tells me anything about her."

"She was a whore."

"That's what I suspected."

"In my own whorehouse. Is that what you needed to

know? She was beautiful. An angel and a gold mine. I'm proud of her."

"I should hope so," Skelton managed.

"Okay," said his father, "what are you going to do?"

"What I said I was."

"That's what I thought."

"What are you going to do?"

"Go back to the house and have a shower and wait and hope to see you again."

The two men walked out of the building under the portraits of Count Zeppelin and the airship *Hansa*. The sun had begun to rise. In half a day, it would drop into the sea before a cheering throng at Mallory dock. Footloose, deracinated tourists, moving coordinates on a thousand chamber-of-commerce war maps, would soon percolate into the density of downtown side streets.

Skelton and his father parted with minimal ceremony. These trips to the hole had been exhausting. Soon they would be looking askance again. Each of them knew that what is perhaps least appropriate in our drumming, cursory march across the glacier is our feckless sense of progress.

SLIPPAGE, DAYDREAMS: THE EYE IS ALMOST never on the ball. Skelton could not go to the bathroom. If you plug up a man's ass, he thought, you will finally shut off his brain. He recalled his old figments, Don and Stacy, the People of the Plains. A knock on the door of their flatlands house. Stacy calls: "Don?"

"What?"

"There is somebody out here with a terrible swift sword."

Tomorrow morning, he was taking Olie Slatt, Montana strip-miner, out to get a trophy.

"LET'S GO OUT TO DINNER."

"Where?" Miranda asked. Skelton named a good place for sea food. "Really," said Miranda.

"What do you mean by that?"

"The stone crab is always cooked too long and it gets mushy. The red snapper is flecked with barf. They use paint thinner on the salad."

"What kind of soap is this?"

"Pine tar," she said.

"We'll smell like a lumberyard. How come it has this cord hooked onto it? So you can retrieve it if you swallow it?"

Skelton pushed one of his feet, invisible under the sudsy water, into Miranda's crotch and gently explored her interior with his toes. "Are you still loaded?"

"Not too."

"What'd you do in school?"

"We all told our best true stories."

"What were the best ones?"

"One boy caught a rattlesnake swimming in the channel at Little Torch . . . I can't think of any more . . ."

"What's wrong."

"I'm afraid about you."

"Don't be."

"I'd plead if I thought it would do any good."

"It wouldn't."

"I still don't see why you think this is a matter of conviction when it's just an extended bar fight."

"That's where you're wrong. It's not a fight at all."

"Well, if you're going to guide tomorrow, I'm going

up to the mainland to see my grandmother. I don't even want to be on the key. And I can't *stand* my grandmother!"

"You've got school. You can't leave."

"I don't care."

"You'll lose your job."

"So what."

"Can I come down to your end?" She said that he could. Skelton slithered around to the opposite end of the tub, displacing so much water that a roller traveled all the way up over the overflow, causing an enormous vomiting noise from the plumbing.

"I want some key lime pie," Skelton said with a smile.

"Maybe not, if you're going to guide."

"Doctor Irving Marfak says in *Key Lime Pie without Tears* that it should never be used to bargain with."

"All right."

"All right what?"

"Pie time."

"Then stop crying."

MIRANDA DROVE UP A1A ALL THE WAY TO ALLI-gator Alley, using the Homestead cutoff to save some time. She couldn't seem to even listen to the radio. After Key West, it was always surprising to see the vegetable stands, the tomato and bean fields; and the straggling agricultural life that transpired on the edge of the 'glades. She was not surprised any more than she listened to the radio.

The beginning of Miranda's stay with her grandmother was like the middle and the end of her stay with her grandmother. Miranda arrived in time for dinner; and her grandmother, a famous social lady, and author of a book about the shells of Sanibel and Captiva islands called *The Bivalve and Me*, was wearing a floor-length dinner dress. She carried a chain bag and a dog.

She was drunk as a skunk.

From time to time, as Miranda readied herself for the dinner upon which she did not have her mind, the dog threw itself at her snapping and snarling. The dog's name was Vecky, short for Carl Van Vechten, and he looked like a wasted rat of imprecise morals.

"Grandmother," said Miranda evenly, "get this animal away from me or I'll take something to its head." Miranda's grandmother showed her disapproval of Miranda. She permitted her lower eyelids to sag farther and farther—quite far actually—until there were considerable red bands of disapproval beneath each of her goo-goo eyes. She was never sure of her footing when she was looped; so she wore the floor-length dresses to hide her basketball shoes. Everyone knew anyway because they could hear their mad squeegee tread as she swept across the room.

They neither of them ate their dinners at the club but hung disconsolate over plates of expensive meat upon which only the bright parsley could draw the eye. The room, it seemed to Miranda, was cast in bluish gloom; in its middle a baby spotlight gave an ice mountain with its shrimp avalanche an unnatural prominence.

Ultimately, Miranda's grandmother called to the waiter in a gravel command voice.

"Klaus! Klaus! Klaus!"

Klaus ran at them; so that others might enjoy their dinners.

"Klaus," she said, "Vecky's heart would be broken." A broad executive gesture passed over the inviolate meat. "What do you say to a bowser bag?"

"Immediately, Missussss Cole."

Some grave force carried Klaus to the kitchen. He emerged shortly with the bowser and, positioning himself to look down Miranda's blouse, he rammed the beef home. Later, Miranda watched the little beast growling in defense of this world of meat, bloodying his bald narrow paws, and running his sliver of tongue through the fat.

WHEN PEEWEE KNOWLES RETURNED FROM Cuba, he spent a week in political quarantine watched by a mongoose from Central Intelligence, watched and questioned and obliged to fill out profiles until his actual nauseating footling politics were triangulated. The Central Intelligence man, who turned out, oddly enough, to be named Don and who was, weird thing, from the Plains states, totaled up the numerical equivalents of Peewee's responses and evaluations. Don's manner with a column of numbers was not unlike that of Myron Moorhen; and when he came up with his total, he divided it by the index number of 10, checked his figures, rose to his feet, and told Peewee he was a Great American.

Peewee headed for Burdine's and bought the complete Arnold Palmer dress ensemble; then sloped to the barbershop in the shopping plaza. "Where did you get your last haircut?" asked the barber. "Key West?"

Peewee turned to him, stared, and said, "No clippers in the back."

When the little insurance man returned to the island city and rejoined his great wife, he was surprised to find himself set upon once more by collection agents. Peewee grew hot around the collar. He was fit to be tied. Soon, however, by selling insurance himself rather than only adjusting, Peewee began to perceive a light at the end of the tunnel. And somewhere along in there, Peewee heard what no married man wants to hear: that, in his absence, the little woman had been putting out.

His first response was an unkind joke. He told Bella that before he'd consider making the love with her again, he would have to slam a five-pound picnic ham in her twat and pull out the bone. Bella gave him a good thrashing for that one.

A day later, Peewee was storming across Key West toward the Skelton Building on Eaton. Goldsboro Skelton was either going to buy a Homeowner's, a Premium Endowment, and a costly Life, or Peewee was *going to know the reason why.*

"I'm here to see Mr. Goldsboro Skelton."

"I'll ring him," said Bella.

Peewee entered Skelton's office.

"How much of that jazz am I going to have to buy?" Goldsboro Skelton inquired of the American. Then just to show Skelton who he was dealing with, Peewee Knowles wrote out a check for a thousand dollars and lit his cigar with it.

That night Peewee entered Bella from beneath, figuring forth the rising aspirations that newly filled his breast like a thousand angry penguins. As for Bella, she lowered herself upon Peewee with a rubicund sense of her own age and history that soon had the temporarily forgotten Peewee calling for air.

SKELTON LAID HIS FEAR IN LIKE SUPPLIES. UP before the sun, he had the gear on his bed, his Polaroids hanging around his neck on monofilament. No wind yet; trees still in the dark; one or two lights on next door.

What does that strip-miner want to eat. He will eat what I give him. Skelton made four liver-sausage and onion sandwiches and put them in the wooden box with oranges and a six-pack of Gator Ade. Tackle was in the boat. Shrimp were in the live wells: six dozen chum, four dozen bait. He had to keep his eye on the ball: a trophy for Olie Slatt.

Ready. Skelton walked around the inside of the fuselage, opened his books with their pages of magic animals; he glanced at his own jejune speculations on DNA replication, graphs in Thompson on the variability of error, a sketch of hypertrophied feathers and prehensile fingers buried in whale flippers: his private, lost science.

THERE IS SOMETHING, HE THOUGHT, THAT I AM tired of.

Breakfast at Shorty's: the famous French toast. Open-hearted fry cooks soar under the menu-cyclorama. The waitress with the blue hair cast a discriminating glance into the doughnut cabinet.

A black gentleman, the only other customer, slid the sugar bowl down the counter to Skelton with exquisite judgment of distance. Skelton fell in love with him. The other waitress, a blond indifferent trull, refilled Skelton's coffee without his asking. He fell in love with her; and mooned between his two new paramours while his Shorty's famous French toast chilled and glazed under a glossy patina of syrup.

I am in love, thought Skelton, though his glances seemed to embarrass both objects of his ardor.

Now let's get over that and read the tide book so we will know where the trophies mean to be today.

TIDE TABLES

High and low water predictions

EAST COAST OF NORTH AND SOUTH AMERICA

INCLUDING GREENLAND

He opened the book and stared at it a few long moments before realizing he didn't need the predictions for Isla Zapara, Venezuela. Idly he eliminated Savannah River entrance, Galveston, and St. John, New Brunswick.

Key West, wintertime, was on page 122. He found his date and read:

0024	0.8
0518	0.0
1142	1.7
1906	0.7

With the three-hour Gulf lag at the Barracudas, he could have good early-incoming water first thing in the morning; then drop back to the Snipes on the West side of Turkey Basin; then Mud Keys, Harbor Keys, Bay Keys, Mule-and-Archer for the long shot on permit, and home; presumably, with a trophy for Olie Slatt to snow his neighbors with.

With that settled, Skelton began to fall out of love. He looked into the street and watched a chromed, rusting Chrysler Imperial glide by, and thought: How terribly depressing. Such an Imperial might rut its lust upon a Dodge Coronet, jetting transmission fluid into our roadway.

"The sun just doesn't half seem to want to come up," he said to the man down the counter, his spirit sinking quick.

"No, sure don't," said the man with a chuckle and holding his breath in case he should need to go on. The waitress said to Skelton, "You want to buy a Studebaker?"

"No. But thanks for asking."

"Huh?"

Skelton's hand, resting in his lap, began to feel for the boat keys; and not discovering them immediately he jumped to his feet and slapped at his pockets, quickly finding them. He sat down again.

It was time to head for the dock. The bill came to $1.40. Skelton had a twenty; he tucked it with the check under his coffee cup. The waitress came up.

"That's good," he said.

"I don't get it."

"Isn't that enough for you?"

Skelton dug in his mouth with his fork and pried out the loose gold inlay, which he set upon the twenty and the check which enumerated French toast and coffee.

"Tell me when you've got enough," he said.

"I've got enough," she said.

"I can't hear you."

"I've got enough," she said, somewhat louder. She was as white as the powdered jelly bismarcks behind her. There was something that Skelton was tired of.

"Who *was* that masked man?" asked the customer who had slid Skelton the sugar.

"I think he's a guide."

"He's not right in the noggin."

"You can say that again."

"He's not right in the noggin."

"Ha-ha!"

The waitress liked to laugh; she sidled down the counter with half a mind to divvy up the inlay. She thought the customer was a real scream.

"MY MAN HERE?"

"Not yet," said Carter. Skelton climbed into the skiff and stowed the lunch. "Cart, grab me a block of ice, would you." Carter brought the block in the tongs and swung it down from the dock; Skelton got the handle and eased the ice into the insulated box. It was too high. Carter handed him the ice pick and he chipped away, ice splintering and flying all over, until the lid would close. He tore the soft drinks from their cardboard and arrayed them around the ice block.

"What are you going to fish for?"

"I'm going to bonefish," Skelton said. "I've got bonefish tides and I'm going to fish them. If Roy Rogers doesn't want to bonefish, he can fuck off."

"I've got a permit charter."

"Well, you got the wrong goddamn tides."

"I know, I know. What's the matter with you?"

Skelton started shouting: "Why do these people want a guide? They can't read tide tables but they already know what they want to fish for!"

"Boy, are you het up. Do like I do; make your moves until four o'clock; then run home and take his money."

Olie Slatt arrived in a taxicab. He was wearing a men's bikini and carrying a terrycloth beach bag. He was complected right for mine life and so it made a certain amount of abstract sense when he donned a bathrobe that came to the ground. He climbed aboard.

"I want a trophy."

Skelton took the beach bag from him to stow it; inside were wrap-around La Dolce Vita sunglasses, a telephone book, bath clogs, and a roll of toilet paper.

So far Nichol Dance hadn't shown. Carter's people were around. First an anesthesiologist and a tool designer from Spokane who were fishing tomorrow; they wanted a brief casting lesson so they could practice up, a task compounded by a certain lack of simple motor control in either of them.

Then today's customers arrived: the Rudleighs, who had abandoned Dance as "a nut case"; old pros in whites and deck shoes, they brought personal tackle boxes and two thermoses of Gibsons.

Skelton started the engine, warmed up briefly, and headed for the ocean. Carter watched him until he saw the skiff jump on plane, then turn downwind toward the backcountry.

Nichol Dance arrived about five minutes later. The Rudleighs backed away.

"We just sent off a guide on his maiden voyage," said Carter.

"Don't say."

"Looked real organized. Had his lunch and gear all clean and layed out and rigged."

"What's he and that snake doctor out for?"

"Bonefish I believe . . ."

Dance nodded toward the two Rudleighs. "You fishing that lunchmeat, Cart?"

"Till four o'clock."

"What kind of tides we got?"

"Five-eighteen Key West low."

"That'd make the Barracuda Keys first stop for the new guide."

"I suppose."

Dance looked at Carter and laughed at him. "Where else? Toptree Hammock? Boy stole half that pattern off me."

Dance was wearing a blue shirt with white dolphins all over it; short-sleeved, outside his pants. Dance was not robustly built but his strong arms made him look like a sport of some kind, a handball player, say.

Cart put his charter aboard and Dance got in his own skiff. Carter came out with a pack of cigarettes; he stopped on the dock and looked at Dance and tore the red thin strip of cellophane from the pack.

Then Dance's engine wouldn't start. Cart came over and primed it for him, pulled the plugs, replaced them, and then succeeded Dance in failing to start it.

"It ain't gonna run," he said, "I can hear it."

Dance said in a vacuum, "Man oh man."

"Do you want to borrow my skiff?" Carter asked him. Dance looked up; Carter was looking elsewhere.

"Do you want to borrow my gun?"

"No."

"Then what do you want to lend me your skiff for?"

"I thought you could use it."

"If I take your skiff, how are you going to pay for that cunt of yours' shopping?"

"I don't know."

"I'm sorry, Cart. I am. I'm sorry I said that."

"Nichol, my clients can see how upset you are."

"All right, all right I'll stop."

"What do you want to do?" Carter asked again, resting his eyes on the highway, ticking off traffic, flow and volume.

"I don't know what I want to do."

"Do you want the skiff?"

"Yes, I'm going to take it."

Carter and Dance walked up the dock to Carter's boat. The Rudleighs were in the skiff now, lounging in the fighting chairs.

"Mister and Missus Rudleigh, can I ask you to get out please?"

The two climbed out bewildered.

"What's up, Captain?"

"My friend needs the skiff. It's looking more like miniature golf today."

Rudleigh said, "Run it past us again, Captain, you were real unclear the first time."

"I'm afraid our fishing is off. We have a kind of emergency to see to."

"Well, we'll be heading directly to the Chamber of

Commerce," said Rudleigh. "Do you have an official version of the event you'd like us to relay as to why a month-old date to fish was canceled?"

"Yes, I do."

"What is it?"

"The captain—or guide—experienced a sudden loss of interest—or ambition—and flaked out without warning."

DANCE WAS GONE IN A ROAR.

"HONEY," CALLED SKELTON'S FATHER TO HIS mother from the bathroom, "scramble me four eggs and pour my coffee now so it will cool."

He shaved very carefully and very thoroughly, preparing his face with a hot washcloth, brushing on the lather thick and hot, then drew stripes through the stubbled foam.

The conversion was quite startling; and once more the slightly olive skin was visible drawn across the facial bones that were those of an Iberian poet who was moved to verse only by a landscape with one tree and a full moon. Just as true, it was the face, if one believed such things, of someone incapable of cruelty; and deeply prone to folly.

He finished shaving, manicured his nails, combed his hair, and dressed for the day in one brisk motion after another; then strolled in for breakfast, which he ate while jotting notes to himself on a pad.

Today he was going to start something. He was trying to work it out on his pad, where he had written:

1. Fire
2. Air

He was still working on 7. It was his lucky number. He couldn't decide between "Infinity" and "Waste Disposal."

"I FEEL AWFUL ABOUT THAT BOY," SAID JEAN-nie when she knew Dance had the boat.

"Why?"

"Because he is going to be killed!"

"Oh, Jeannie please. Nichol won't hurt him."

"What do you think he's out there to do!"

Carter was thumb-indenting a neat four-in-hand for his visit to the Chamber of Commerce.

"Kill himself," he said, "that seems pretty plain to me." Then for the thousandth time he began to explain that no force on earth could keep a man from doing away with himself if that was what he was bound and determined to do. He checked the tie in the mirror; then raised his eyes to his own and thought: *You are a hamster on a wheel and a low-breed dog in one.*

"Jeannie, let's us go out and buy something big."

"Why hon?"

"Come on. Something big as all suicide to stand in the lawn. I think it should be some bright color or something to match the shutters." Her face fell.

"No, you," she said, frightening Carter for maybe the first time. "I think it's something you should buy."

It was a tough and gnarled remark that they would both get over; Jeannie would get over it first, deploying her bruised spirit among the New Year sales and One

Time Only offers; first-to-come Jeannie would be the first served; until that undetermined hour when she is precipitated into the hole with the rest of us.

THE FLATS APPENDING THE NORTHWEST END of the Barracuda Keys form a connection between that minute archipelago and Snipe Point. They are, in effect, the western rim of Turkey Basin, diurnally drawing two great sweeps of ocean across the turtle-grass flats, dividing the bank into beveled sections; which from the air resemble scarabs of an annealed green next to the sky-stained green of the Gulf of Mexico. Along the inner rim, there is a concentration of large and hazardous niggerheads.

Skelton started fishing the first of these flats on the incoming water, poling down light toward Snipe Point. They found four schools of bonefish on the first flat coming in with sting rays, bonnet sharks, and small cudas. They found two schools on the second flat, tailing on the edge of the creek and making a thirty- or forty-foot mud. Olie Slatt hooked his trophy in this second school, an exceptional bonefish. They drifted in on the tide while they fought the fish and Skelton boated it among the niggerheads.

He could hear Dance's skiff the last ten minutes of the fight, but poled Slatt in on his prize and netted it succinctly. Dance ran right in on them and cut his engine. He climbed into Skelton's boat with the gun in his hand and asked Skelton where he wanted it. Skelton pointed to the place he had imagined at the shopping plaza some time ago. And the question of his conviction or courage was answered. But this was not theater; and Dance shot him through the heart anyway. It was the discovery of his life.

Dance gave Slatt the heavy gun and sat in the bottom of the skiff next to Skelton.

Instead of shooting Dance, which is what Slatt first thought he owed the republic, Slatt hit him over the head a sledge blow with the gun. He kept hitting until he felt the head jelly under his blows. The empty skiff began to fall with the tide toward the sea.

Then he started the engine. He ran standing up, with Skelton and Dance, two foiled and strangely synchronous lives, in a pile at his feet. The white robe he wore carried behind him and he held the bright trophy to his chest. His jaws were parted slightly to the rush of air.

He was heading for A1A.

FOR THE BEST IN PAPERBACKS, LOOK FOR THE

In every corner of the world, on every subject under the sun, Penguin represents quality and variety—the very best in publishing today.

For complete information about books available from Penguin—including Pelicans, Puffins, Peregrines, and Penguin Classics—and how to order them, write to us at the appropriate address below. Please note that for copyright reasons the selection of books varies from country to country.

In the United Kingdom: For a complete list of books available from Penguin in the U.K., please write to *Dept E.P., Penguin Books Ltd, Harmondsworth, Middlesex, UB7 0DA.*

In the United States: For a complete list of books available from Penguin in the U.S., please write to *Dept BA, Penguin*, Box 120, Bergenfield, New Jersey 07621-0120.

In Canada: For a complete list of books available from Penguin in Canada, please write to *Penguin Books Canada Ltd, 10 Alcorn Avenue, Suite 300, Toronto, Ontario, Canada M4V 3B2.*

In Australia: For a complete list of books available from Penguin in Australia, please write to the *Marketing Department, Penguin Books Ltd, P.O. Box 257, Ringwood, Victoria 3134.*

In New Zealand: For a complete list of books available from Penguin in New Zealand, please write to the *Marketing Department, Penguin Books (NZ) Ltd, Private Bag, Takapuna, Auckland 9.*

In India: For a complete list of books available from Penguin, please write to *Penguin Overseas Ltd, 706 Eros Apartments, 56 Nehru Place, New Delhi, 110019.*

In Holland: For a complete list of books available from Penguin in Holland, please write to *Penguin Books Nederland B.V., Postbus 195, NL-1380AD Weesp, Netherlands.*

In Germany: For a complete list of books available from Penguin, please write to *Penguin Books Ltd, Friedrichstrasse 10-12, D-6000 Frankfurt Main I, Federal Republic of Germany.*

In Spain: For a complete list of books available from Penguin in Spain, please write to *Longman, Penguin España, Calle San Nicolas 15, E-28013 Madrid, Spain.*

In Japan: For a complete list of books available from Penguin in Japan, please write to *Longman Penguin Japan Co Ltd, Yamaguchi Building, 2-12-9 Kanda Jimbocho, Chiyoda-Ku, Tokyo 101, Japan.*

FOR THE BEST IN CONTEMPORARY AMERICAN FICTION

☐ **WHITE NOISE**
  Don DeLillo

The New Republic calls *White Noise* "a stunning performance from one of our most intelligent novelists." This masterpiece of the television age is the story of Jack Gladney, a professor of Hitler Studies in Middle America, whose life is suddenly disrupted by a lethal black chemical cloud.

          326 pages   ISBN: 0-14-007702-2

☐ **IRONWEED**
  William Kennedy

William Kennedy's Pulitzer Prize-winning novel is the story of Francis Phelan — ex-ball-player, part-time gravedigger, and full-time drunk.

          228 pages   ISBN: 0-14-007020-6

☐ **LESS THAN ZERO**
  Bret Easton Ellis

This phenomenal best-seller depicts in compelling detail a generation of rich, spoiled L.A. kids on a desperate search for the ultimate sensation.

          208 pages   ISBN: 0-14-008894-6

☐ **THE LAST PICTURE SHOW**
  Larry McMurtry

In a small town in Texas during the early 1950s, two boys act out a poignant drama of adolescence — the restless boredom, the bouts of beer-drinking, and the erotic fantasies.   *220 pages   ISBN: 0-14-005183-X*

☐ **THE WOMEN OF BREWSTER PLACE**
A Novel in Seven Stories
Gloria Naylor

Winner of the American Book Award, this is the story of seven survivors of an urban housing project — a blind alley feeding into a dead end. From a variety of backgrounds, they experience, fight against, and sometimes transcend the fate of black women in America today.

192 pages   *ISBN: 0-14-006690-X*

☐ **STONES FOR IBARRA**
Harriet Doerr

An American couple comes to the small Mexican village of Ibarra to reopen a copper mine, learning much about life and death from the deeply faithful villagers.   *214 pages*   *ISBN: 0-14-007562-3*

☐ **WORLD'S END**
T. Coraghessan Boyle

"Boyle has emerged as one of the most inventive and verbally exuberant writers of his generation," writes *The New York Times*. Here he tells the story of Walter Van Brunt, who collides with early American history while searching for his lost father.   *456 pages*   *ISBN: 0-14-009760-0*

☐ **THE WHISPER OF THE RIVER**
Ferrol Sams

The story of Porter Osborn, Jr., who, in 1938, leaves his rural Georgia home to face the world at Willingham University, *The Whisper of the River* is peppered with memorable characters and resonates with the details of place and time. Ferrol Sams's writing is regional fiction at its best.

528 pages   *ISBN: 0-14-008387-1*

☐ **ENGLISH CREEK**
Ivan Doig

Drawing on the same heritage he celebrated in *This House of Sky,* Ivan Doig creates a rich and varied tapestry of northern Montana and of our country in the late 1930s.   *338 pages*   *ISBN: 0-14-008442-8*

☐ **THE YEAR OF SILENCE**
Madison Smartt Bell

A penetrating look at the varied reactions to a young woman's suicide exactly one year later, *The Year of Silence* "captures vividly and poignantly the chancy dance of life." (*The New York Times Book Review*)

208 pages   *ISBN: 0-14-011533-1*